T0078453

Destiny

Only an invincible love can change a destiny

Kerrine E. Peck

Order this book online at www.trafford.com
or email orders@trafford.com

Most Trafford titles are also available at major online book retailers.

Printed in the United States of America.

ISBN: 978-1-4669-9923-7 (sc)
ISBN: 978-1-4669-9922-0 (e)

Trafford rev. 11/20/2014

Trafford
PUBLISHING   www.trafford.com

North America & international
toll-free: 1 888 232 4444 (USA & Canada)
fax: 812 355 4082

ACKNOWLEDGMENTS

This is Kerrine Peck's first book, and it would not have been possible without her mom and dad for their inspiration. She will be always grateful for giving her the head start to get her writing out and in the hands of her readers around the world. She would like to say a big thank you in believing in her and the production of this book.

Foremost, she would like to thank Sarah England, whom she is very lucky to have, such a brilliant friend for her help and useful criticism on the book. Some characters are fictional except her grandmother, whom she greatly loved and respected.

What is your dream?

The majority of people like to dream with faith and perseverance,

especially if one is motivated by positive feelings.

Destiny is not given to us, but it is the path we choose for

ourselves, knowing your dream and living it—this is the whole

purpose behind simplifying your life.

PROLOGUE

*I*n the summer of 1989, on one of the magnificent Islands of the Antilles, with its beautiful, exotic white sandy beaches, spectacular enormous mountains that seem to touch the sky, looking over the clear waters, and sunbathers relax, where they can sit and watch the sun rise and set. You will feel the warmth of its people and the weather during the months of June to August; it becomes warmer. It is the fairest island eyes have beheld. The city, however, is a charming mix of many fine old buildings, classic eighteenth-century Georgian mansions and some hugely expensive houses for the tourists, apartment blocks, restaurants, gift shops, and galleries. It also has appealing slums, especially in the western part. About a few miles away from the city, you can relax and breathe deeply and take time to enjoy life in Mere Wood Village, with its fourteen thousand inhabitants, including farmers. A farmer's life is not easy. They have some social differences of ethnicity and lifestyle choices, creating two separate groups of families that experienced prejudice, discrimination, and oppression in various forms that influence today. There were not so many wooden houses because this magical island is still surrounded by its lush green vegetation. That is the first thing that attracts your attention when you arrive either by boat or by plane, and around there, everybody knows everything about everyone in the neighbourhood.

On this island lives an extraordinarily beautiful young woman named Sheena. She is in her late twenties, with exciting exotic features; she is five feet seven inches in height and has a slim and delicate figure, with black Indian silk hair that is almost shoulder-length and dark eyes that seem to hold all the mysteries in the universe. She lives with her entire family—a large family of seven children, for her the family always comes first—not far from the sea in the area lined with trees. Sheena is the youngest member of the family. Everyone who knows her will say she is a typical girl from the country but enjoys going out like the rest of her friends. She has never travelled abroad and has always wondered what it would be like to live outside, like many individuals who have fled from the island. She has heard so many rumours about Canada, England, and America, its democracy, freedom, and liberty. Nevertheless, her parents, especially her father, a handsome caring man, had a strict moral code.

Her father adores her. He would spoil her and tell her how beautiful she looked and compliment her on her grades, her behaviour, and her friends. She would work alongside her grandma, Datilda, a sweet, loving elderly woman, age seventy-five, who sells homemade articles and fruits in a sunny outdoor market downtown. Sheena was very unhappy, living just one type of life on the island.

She wished she were somewhere else. This is not where the female protagonist thought she would be. There was no thought of love or story; she never thought that her life would change until she met the dashing Jonathan Samson, who would be interested in an ordinary country girl like her. He was the only son of one of the wealthiest businessmen in Seattle; he was twenty-nine, dashing, white, tall—with a body sculpted with muscles, short-cut blond hair, and hazel blue eyes—and immature for his age. At the age of seven, he spent a lot of time with adults and his grandparents. In particular, Joseph Murphy Richardson was his favourite until he died. At twenty-seven, he had just finished his studies at university; and the next step, according to his parents, was to work alongside his father in the company and attend host charities, organize VIP fundraising dinners and to marry someone wealthy. The very thought of marriage made him feel uneasy. He hardly sees his father, and the relationship between the two was not easy. He loved the life he had; he loved the lifestyle that he was accustomed to but hated the attention and obligations that came along with it. Jonathan and Sheena had nothing whatsoever in common.

Soon he was working for his father and was the future owner of the Samson Company. For the next few days, nothing much happened. Jonathan got up every morning at about the same time and went through his usual routine, getting dressed, going to work, slaving away in the office, going home, eating his dinner at home with his mother or going out with friends in town or the city, and going to bed. Jonathan senses loneliness in his family, though his parents' marriage is a happy one. This is not where the two protagonists thought their ambition would lie, but somehow they have ended up here, living a life of greed, loneliness, poverty, or materialism. They know that there was something missing in their lives, but they did not know what. Almost immediately, they are attracted; and through their love, Jonathan began to find happiness and meaning in his life. Their brief but passionate love story is slowly threatened, but soon a hidden secret is revealed. Their families have had a raging feud that began with their great-grandfathers, revealed by Sheena's grandmother. Sheena and Jonathan pretend not to mind their family's violent history but concentrate on the joy they found with each other until the situation starts to get out of hand with Jonathan's father, Steven Samson.

CHAPTER ONE

*I*t is the beginning of summer 1989, and it is the most important time of the year. Everything good and everything magical happens between the months of June and August. But this summer, it was the summer when everything began differently. On one lazy day on the beach, with Cattleya, Jalissa, and Shakeia, Sheena sat down and gazed out over the Caribbean Sea, feeling the faint breeze and enjoying the warmth of the sun on her face, shading her eyes with one hand, the white sand warm between her bare toes. The place was beautiful beyond belief. In a few hours, the beach would be packed with tourists lying on their towels in the hot sun, soaking up the rays. She got up and walked to the water's edge to let the tiny waves lap over her feet. The water was refreshing, but the beauty around her was unable to ease the grief she felt for her grandmother, who took badly ill of a heart attack. Sheena was asked by her family to take her grandmother's place in the market, putting aside her plans to finish university and stay home, where she was needed until Datilda was in better health. Later in the afternoon at the market, while the sun slanted down, Sheena was dazed for a moment, thinking what it would be like to live outside her little island and hoped one day she too will leave the island like many before her.

After a day's work in the market, every afternoon at half past four, Sheena decided to go for a relax in her natural quiet spot, away from everyone and everything, just to appreciate what life had to offer in her natural swimming pool. Here she could relax, listening to the rustling of leaves between the tropical plants, the splash of water tumbling over the rocks. She lifts her eyes and stares up into the clear blue sky, listening to the calls and singing tunes of birds in the trees, such place we would call paradise because of its clear transparent water. Soon, she started to set back home as it was getting late. Following the path home in the moonlight, she began to ask herself while walking again, "What must it be like outside? Would it be better or worse?"

The following morning, sun struck the edge of Sheena's pillow with potent brilliance. Sheena woke up by the chirps and twitters of the early risers out of the doors. A bird looked in through the window and tapped with its beak on the glass.

"Sheena! Wake up!" her mother called out from below.

She slid out of the bed and walked over to the window. Far below her window was her dog running around. A faint white cloud moved slowly past her window in the serene blue sky. She could have gazed out her window for hours, but she had to get dressed and ready; it was another day at the market, selling her grandmother's goods. The heat was unbearable; women were waving their fans to keep cool.

When the day was over, she would start her journey toward her secret place. It was a long walk, and she loved every minute of it despite the heat. For weeks, this continued until one day, among her friends, the trees, and the singing tunes of birds, she saw a tall young figure in the pool, swimming. He was white with short-cut blond hair. She stopped, and she quickly hid herself behind a plant which had big broad leaves and stared at the figure in the water. "Who is he?" she asked herself. As she stepped back a little, not noticing that there was a large chunk of rock, she stumbled over and fell backward, toward a large bush which made a sound. Jonathan, hearing a slight noise behind him, turned his head to see who or what it was.

"Who's there?" he shouted out. He couldn't see anything, only plants and trees around the pool. He went back to relax himself by swimming in the water. Then he heard the sound again. This time, he looked around. Something ran quickly away, and he stared. It was a woman, a young woman. Sheena was afraid that she turned and ran away, but one of her sandals came off her feet. She did not go back to get it; she was so afraid that she hurried all the way home.

From a far distance, Coretta saw her running so fast toward her. "Sheena, why are you running?" asked Coretta laughing. "You're running as if a wild pig is after you."

Sheena stopped and walked slowly over to her. "Err . . . ," she mumbled. At first, Sheena did not know what to say, and then she began to think clearly so as not to worry her. She looked at her. "Nothing . . . I just felt worried about Grandma. I wanted to come home as quickly as possible."

"Her heart attack wasn't a bad one, child. Trust me, she'll be all right. She's resting easily now. I'll go with your father to the hospital and see when she'll be able to come home." Her mother hugged her, and they both walked toward the house, leaving the rest of the family outside.

In the meantime, back at the pool, Jonathan decided to leave. After dressing himself, he slung his jacket over his shoulder, moving silently among the leaves and dry twigs lying on the ground near some bushes where he heard the noise. A dry twig snapped; he spotted something. He bent down and found there, behind a clump of bushes on his left where the girl evidently had been hiding, a sandal. He picked it up and looked at it; he took it with him and placed it in his jeep, parked at the edge of the woods. He climbed in and made his way home.

After some time, Sheena's grandmother was feeling better and was able to return to the market. During their long walks together from the outdoor market downtown to their house, Sheena could see from a far distance a tall white figure approaching. As they were getting closer, she realized it was the young man whom she saw in the pool. Her heart began to beat so fast because she was afraid if the young man saw her that day. Gradually, as they both were getting closer, Sheena's heart was beating faster and faster with fear. She lowered her head to avoid looking at him. As they crossed each other's path, she could not help herself having a quick glimpse of him. Sheena's grandmother, Datilda, stopped the young man who was passing by and asked if he wanted to buy something from her. As he answered, he could not help himself not to stare at the young woman. He was immediately struck by her beauty. His heart pounded and felt himself grow hot. She was in fact one of the most beautiful young women he had ever seen, with silk skin shining in the sun; her eyes were big and black; her shoulders were slim; her lips were much to be desired; and her hair was long, silk deep black like her eyes.

At first, Jonathan did not know who they were in reality, but even if he had known, it would not have been important. Datilda presented herself to the young man, knowing who he was. "And this is my granddaughter, Sheena Becker, and I am her grandmother, Datilda Shawn."

To cover his nervousness, he coughed then murmured, "Pleased to meet you. I'm American."

A delicious smell was suddenly shifting in the air-freshly baked bread and bun. He inhaled then sniffed.

"What's that smell?" he asked as he looked down. "I can see that you have some things in your basket that smells delicious."

It was the scent of fresh baked buns loaded with cinnamon. Sheena smiled at him.

"Yes," responded Datilda. "I sell homemade things. I have bun and bread that I baked this morning. It's still warm. Would you like a piece?" she asked. She pretended as if she did not know who he was. "And you?" Datilda asked. "What do you do?"

"I'm from Seattle," said Jonathan. "My family owns one of the biggest companies in America and here on the island," continued Jonathan. "I haven't had homemade things for a long time. Yes, please," he said. "The last time I did, was when I was a child."

He helped himself to a warm piece of bun and thanked her. "Well, you should both be getting on your way. It's getting late." Jonathan continued, "It was nice talking to you."

"Me too," said Datilda. "Take care of yourself now, you hear." waving her hand with a smile. As they left each other's path, Datilda turned to Sheena saying, "He's a nice young man." Sheena turned around to look at him while he was walking away toward his jeep. As Jonathan reached his jeep, he tried not to glance into his rearview mirror, searching for a final glimpse of her before she disappeared from sight, for he had never seen anyone quite so beautiful.

It was evening with the sun down and food just finished eaten. The family decided to go outside on to the terrace to tell stories. The air was cool and refreshing followed by the noise of field crickets and mosquitoes. This was Sheena's favourite kind of evenings, an evening of dreams and hopes. (*Everyone needed hopes . . . everyone needed dreams. What does a man have if not his dreams?*) In the background, Datilda would always talk about the good old days when she was young, what she used to do, and her husband . . . the sounds of laughter and familiar songs. While Sheena glared at all the shining stars in the sky, admiring the most beautiful scenery that God had created, she felt as if she was in paradise, the cool gentle breeze blowing against her skin slightly, the sound of nature singing, and the perfume of flowers flowing in the breeze. In the background, you could hear Sheena's grandmother singing happily.

CHAPTER TWO

*T*he very next day, in the early afternoon, Leon decided to go visiting family members and friends nearby. As the rest of the family leave with him, Sheena was left with her eldest brother Glenn, their grandmother, and Coretta, her mother. It was quiet without the rest of the family. Datilda called Sheena inside the house to join her outside on the terrace. They both went outside and sat down with a cool ice drink. Rusky the dog barked and ran up and down, the bees buzzing. Datilda began to talk with her, "Well, I am getting old as you can see, and I have lived for a long time. Still, you never know what might happen. Life is full of surprises and shocks, Sheena. You should be thinking about a young person by now," said Datilda. "And when you do find this young person, whoever he may be, he must treat you well, don't forget that," said Datilda.

"Grandma! Don't say these things. You will always be around . . . What would I do without you?" responded Sheena, hugging her.

A car came by, blowing its klaxon. Jalissa, Cattleya, and Shakeia were in the car. The three women were good-looking, but they were strikingly different in appearance and personality. When the car came to a stop, they went over to Sheena to embrace her. Sheena left her grandmother and walked to join them.

"Hi, sweetie! We miss you." They said with smiles on their faces.

"I know, I know. I miss you too," said Sheena, smiling.

"How's your grandma now?" asked Jalissa.

"Oh, she's fine. What's everyone planning to do tonight?" asked Sheena.

"Why don't you come with us tonight?" asked Shakeia.

"I don't know . . . What's new?"

"Oh, come on, Sheena! You cannot just sit around and do nothing. We will pick you up around nine," said Cattleya.

That same evening, a car pulled up out front and honked twice outside Sheena's house. The headlights from the car glided across Sheena's bedroom ceiling. The driver blinked the lights. Jalissa and Cattleya were in the car. Cattleya stepped out. "Come on, Sheena!" she yelled. Sheena, dressed in her best clothes, stepped out. Jalissa stepped out the car and walked over to hug her. After hugging and kissing, they went back into the car a drove off. Shakeia was already there, and some other students from university too. Sheena stepped into the club; she brushed against the crowd. The club was dark, but the grape kaleidoscope illuminated the writhing bodies on the dance floor.

"Hey, girl."

"Hey, Shakeia. Looks like you all got the party started already," Sheena said, trying not to look concerned about time.

"Yep, and drink is on its way," said Shakeia, in an exciting party atmosphere, signalling the barmaid to bring over their drinks. They drink beer and danced all night, then they decided to visit a shabby local bar on the beach and got drunk on coca and rum. At first light, the sun shone bright enough around the house. Sheena's mother was in the yard, plucking the chicken feathers; and the dog, Rusty, was running up and down, playing with the chickens in the yard. Jonathan drove past in his red Tesla; he slowed down and looked at the house from a far distance. Coretta noticed a car and wondered who it was that she asked Sheena if she knew the person. She answered no. She thought he must be a visitor on the island that had lost his way in the country. She got up and walked down toward the gate. "Good morning. Can I do something for you?" Jonathan stopped and introduced himself. Her eyes lit with surprise. There was silence between them for a moment; she turned her back and went away without responding. Jonathan was confused and left without a word.

The next day, in the evening, Leon and the rest of the family were returning home. Coretta rose from where she was sitting and went in to the kitchen to prepare the supper—chicken and red rice with hot spicy sauce. As the family gathered together, sitting at opposite sides of the table, eating slowly, talking to each other. There was a knock at the door. Everybody turned round to see who it was. The oldest son, Glenn, rose from his seat and headed toward the door. He opened the door and found in front of him standing a tall young man. "Evening," Jonathan said.

"Evening, Mr. Samson!" said Glenn, surprised.

"Forgive me if I—" he cut him off.

"What brings you here?" asked Glenn, worried.

"Sorry to bother you. I think this belongs to your family," responded Jonathan.

Jonathan opened a brown paper bag that he had in his hand; Glenn looked inside and saw a sandal that he knew belonged to his younger sister, Sheena. He lifted his eyes and looked at Jonathan puzzled and asked where he found it and how he knew it belonged to his family. Jonathan began to explain. Glenn invited him in the house and took him where the rest of the family was. Approaching the dinner room, which had rumbled with noise where the rest were, Glenn shouted out, "Hey, everybody, look who's here. Come on through." He turned to him.

Leon did not even notice the person his son had brought in because he was lost in thought. The room suddenly became quiet. Leon looked up; every head swung toward Glenn.

"This is Jonathan Samson," Glenn said, introducing him to the family.

"Evening! Sorry to interrupt your evening."

With an expression of surprise, Datilda said, "Backfoot! The nice young man. Come, come and sit here." She placed her hand on a chair next to her. "Come!" repeated Datilda.

Sheena turned round and looked up with surprise to find the young man in her house in front of her. For a second, she felt as if she was going to faint. Jonathan's piercing gaze met hers; it was impossible for either of them to look away. Jonathan had the impression that he lacked the land under his feet. Sheena was the only woman who ever had that effect on him. Sheena felt a strange feeling came over her; she could not figure out what exactly. There was a sudden warmth in her that began somewhere in the chest, and it began to swell within her. She felt lighter than air. The room flickered out of existence, and only she and Jonathan existed in the room. It was as if the world came to a stop without being noticed by any member of the family except for Glenn. She had never felt this way about a man before, and it was an exhilarating experience. Jonathan immediately noticed her. He made her nervous. She had no way of knowing how he felt about her. Leon turned and asked Glenn who the young man was.

"Evening!" replied everyone.

"What his name?" asked Leon.

"You know his name. It's Jonathan Samson. He's the son of Steven Samson. Remember I told you some days ago? I've talked about the promotion," replied Glenn.

"What? Oh! Oh yes." He had no idea what he was talking about. Being distracted, he mistook him for someone else.

Glenn was there to translate the language of his father to help Jonathan understand.

"What brings him here this evening?" Leon asked.

Jonathan approached Leon and said, "I have something to give you which, I do believe, belongs to your daughter . . . I found it," he announced.

In the meantime, Sheena rose from the table, carrying the empty bowls to the kitchen to help her sisters bring other things out on the table. Jonathan could not help himself noticing Sheena leaving the dinner table. In the kitchen, Sheena heard her grandma say, "Eat with us . . . There's plenty of food . . . Don't be shy."

"Yes! Yes! Join us," said everyone.

"No, thank you . . . I don't want to bother you all. I have already eaten . . . Thank you anyway . . . I just came by to give this, I found it," replied Jonathan.

Leon interrupted the conversation. He was confused and suspicious of the way he said it and began to ask more questions. "What do you mean by you believe *it* belongs to my daughter?" Leon asked with anger, "What is going on here . . . is there something that I don't know?"

"No! No!" said Jonathan, trying to explain. "You misunderstood me!" continued Jonathan, trying to explain to Sheena's father. He didn't understand why the tension.

Leon looked inside the bag with curiosity. He saw that there was a single sandal that belongs to Sheena, which he gave to her on her twenty-third birthday. He raised his head and looked at Glenn. "Where did he find it?" Leon was starting to get nervous and started to ask more questions again. "How do you know this belongs to one of my daughters?" asked Leon in an angry tone. Jonathan tried again to explain, but he was not able to make himself clear.

Leon was a strict, respectable, serious man, and, above all, stubborn. As Sheena re-entered the dining room, she sat next to her mother, not knowing what was happening. Leon raised his voice with angry demanding questions. Coretta turned and looked at Sheena.

"What's this I'm hearing, child? Do you know him?" asked Coretta, with a whispering voice. "You know what your father's like."

Everyone around the dinner table looked at her. Sheena was afraid to answer, but with a very low voice, Sheena replied, "I didn't do anything."

"Speak up, child . . . I can't hear you!" said Coretta.

"I didn't do anything," repeated Sheena.

"Then what is it?" asked Coretta.

"Nothing," Sheena replied again.

Leon got up from his chair and approached Jonathan. "GET OUT OF MY HOUSE AND DO NOT RETURN!" he said in a firm voice. He walked over to his daughter, Sheena, leaving Jonathan to see himself out and ordered her to follow him. She rose to her feet and followed him. Jonathan felt so embarrassed. He tried explaining again, but it was no use. He just did not want to hear what he had to say. Glenn arrived and went up to Jonathan.

Glenn turned and walked over to Jonathan, trying to find out what happened and why. Jonathan began to explain what the discussion was all about, "I'm sorry. No, I'm really sorry. I didn't mean to hurt anybody, and I meant no disrespect."

"It wasn't your fault," answered Glenn.

In the meantime, the other members were staring at each other. Coretta ran up to her husband, trying to defend Sheena and to calm him down with a slow, steady voice. "She didn't do anything!" Of course, Coretta realized the error that Sheena had made, not confiding with them. They went toward the lounge. Leon started to shout with anger because he felt betrayed by Sheena's trust. Sheena did not say one word; she was too afraid to open her mouth. Coretta went up to her husband, trying to calm him down and making him realize that he was terrifying his daughter and not letting her speak. Glenn entered the room while everyone else was outside. While Leon was still demanding Sheena to answer his questions, she turned away from him crying and ran toward her room, where she locked herself in so nobody could enter. After a few minutes, Datilda, in the kitchen, could hear her son shouting. She walked out to hear what the commotion was all about. All their heads turned in her direction. She found out that Leon was shouting at his daughter about her sandal while entering the room.

"What's going on here, and why all the shouting?"

She went up to her son and said, "You're a dead stamp of your father, STUBBORN!" wagging her finger at him. "Your pushing your daughter away from you. You're not going to get her to trust you this way."

Glenn approached his father after listening to Jonathan and told his father to listen, trying to calm him and everyone down. He began to explain the whole story to him. Coretta began to remember that day. She noticed that one of her feet was without a sandal. "Yes!" said Coretta, confirming what Glenn had said. "I remember, I even asked why she was running," continued Coretta.

"Now you see," said Datilda, entering the room. "So why all the fuss?" she exclaimed. "How do you expect your daughter to confide in you if you treat her this way!" said Datilda angrily.

Leon began to calm down. He walked toward Sheena's room and knocked on the door, hearing her weeping. He opened the door and walked over toward her and sat beside her on the bed, feeling guilty. Then he began to ask with a different tone of voice.

"Is it true what your brother said?" he asked. "You can speak. I'm not going to shout at you."

"Yes, it's true," she answered.

His arms stretched out to embrace her, asking for her forgiveness. Her mother came into the room and caressed her face, and her grandmother squeezed her cheeks. Jonathan was standing in the hallway with the rest of the family, feeling embarrassed. He saw Sheena and her parents coming from the room. He walked over to her and apologized for what had happened. Sheena looked at him for a second time . . . He was dashing. Leon went in between them, ordering Jonathan to leave. Glenn, placing his hands on Jonathan shoulder as a mean of friendship, advised him to leave and go with him into town. While they both were walking in the town, the air was cool and the atmosphere was lively. The town lights were on; there were a lot of people, tourist, villagers, and townsmen, passing by. Music was coming from local places and open restaurants, with people sitting outside, talking to each other and laughing.

The whole island was preparing for their merrymaking feast, carnival, with their bright colourful costumes, their spectacular floats, and their joy of living. The atmosphere on the island was intense; people were rehearsing while preparing their costumes. There were many orchestras with steel drums, the rhythm and style of the music would touch you, and bring out the emotional feeling within you that made you feel alive. By evening, friends of the family came by to prepare their steel band music. They were fifty in a group, twenty men and five young men and twenty-five fantastic outfits. The music gave a sense of freedom. Only a few more days to go before the big day. The town was full of people from the island and tourists from around the world. The hotels were fully booked. The main streets in which the parade was going to take place were covered with bright ribbons and huts selling drinks and food. That same evening, Jonathan decided to return to Sheena's home. He stopped at the door for a moment and thought before knocking. One of the family members heard a knock at the door and went over and opened it. Drusilla found Jonathan standing in front of her, asking to see Glenn. "Come in!" she said.

As he entered the house, Datilda saw him and said with a smile, "Come! Come! Come with me." Jonathan followed her out into the garden where the rest of the family was. "Look!" shouted Datilda. "The nice young man again," she continued. Everyone turned around; they were surprised to see Jonathan again.

Sheena's father approached Jonathan with a smile to greet him. "What brings you here this evening? Glenn's not here."

"I just had to come to see if things were all right after the problem I caused."

"Ah, okay." Leon sighed.

He invited Jonathan to join them out into the garden, where the rest of the family was listening to the music that they were preparing for their big day until Glenn arrives. Jonathan sat next to Datilda, listening to the sweet melody that was coming from the steel drums.

"It is a fantastic experience to be able to participate in the parade well-known for its creative extravagance and powerful colours," said Datilda. "You don't have to be artistic as you are surrounded by so much inspiration. I think you will love it."

She rose from her seat and walked away, leaving Jonathan sitting alone on a chair. Sheena wanted to talk to him. She was a bit shy. She plucked courage and walked over shyly to apologize for her father. He gazed at her as she walked toward him. He was attracted to her beauty. He had never met a woman so beautifully groomed and well put together.

"I'm pleased to meet you. My name is Sheena, and I apologize for my father's behaviour," she said politely and offered her hand to him. He took it. She noticed his hand was soft, but his grasp was firm.

"I'm happy to meet you too," he murmured. She sat next to him. He was completely unaware that she was glancing at him. She noticed how extremely handsome-looking he was and recognized the sadness in his eyes. Throughout the whole evening, they were talking and laughing. The more she spoke, the better he felt about himself. Coretta and Glenn were wondering what they were saying to each other.

"Can I see you tomorrow?" he asked.

"I don't know," she said shyly with her eyes downcast.

"I was hoping the two of us could get together to become acquainted?"

Looking up at him, she said, "Nooo."

"Can I invite you for lunch with me? I know a good place, or you choose." He flashed a smile.

She opened her eyes very wide. "Are you asking me to dine with you alone?"

"Of course, I am!" he said, smiling.

Sheena laughed. "Thank you for your kind invitation, but no."

"Why?" asked Jonathan.

"If you really want to know the truth, I would never dine with you alone after what everybody is saying about you!"

"What are people saying about me? Is it really as bad as that?" After a moment, he said,

"Okay, I won't insist," he said. Jonathan was enjoying the evening—right up until the moment when Coretta pushed herself into the conversation. It took a moment for his eyes to adjust. Glenn rose from where he was sitting and went over to them.

"What are you guys saying?" Glenn called out suspiciously.

"Nothing," they said in unison.

Glenn then asked Jonathan to join him. When they were steps away, Jonathan turned round and quickly glazed at Sheena while leaving. It was the first time they were near one another. She turned and gave him a shy smile. He had the impression that land was shifting under his feet. Sheena was the only woman who had ever had this effect on him. On their way to town, Glenn began to ask Jonathan questions about his sister. "What do you think about my sister?"

"Which one?" asked Jonathan.

"You know, don't be funny . . . Sheen, the one that you was talking to. Do you like her?" asked Glenn.

"Why?" Jonathan wondered.

"I am asking! That is all," said Glenn.

"Well, she's beautiful and very shy," he said.

"I have noticed how you looked at her this evening," said Glenn. "I think she likes you."

"How would you know?"

"The way she looks at you," he said.

Jonathan kept quiet for a while. He did not know what to say. He felt embarrassed, and at the same time, he denied what Glenn said as if he did not understand what Glenn intended, but he knew that he was attracted to her.

CHAPTER THREE

*I*t was the big day; Jonathan woke up early in the morning, lay on his bed wide awake, thinking as he lay staring at the ceiling. He envisioned Sheena's face in his mind, projected her image on the ceiling. He realized that his attraction to her was powerful. He was tired living a life that had no sense. Most of all, he was tired of doing the same old things and, one in particular, not being able to talk with his father. Being distracted by the thoughts of Sheena, he said to himself, "I can't resist her. I must get to know her." He knew her name, but he could not call her.

He got out of bed and prepared himself. It was hot too, partying people all taking to the streets, and the parades were crowded too with plenty of dancers in their extravagantly colourful costumes and many orchestras and the sounds of steel bands playing their music. Carnival—a time of excitement and fun in the sun. This hot and exciting event comes around only once a year. Beautiful decorated lights were hung throughout the whole streets. The people were enjoying a series of parades with their amazing floats, jumping up and down in the streets, dancing along with the parade in their skimpy, magnificent, colourful, and sometimes daring outfits like the Queen of the Battery, dressed in fantastic peacock outfits and others of glittering colours of all sizes and shapes. Blowing whistles and shouting to the fun-loving music, the atmosphere was so intense! Sheena, full of life and energy, was so happy, singing joyfully, dancing in her costume with her friends, Jalissa, Shakeia, and Cattleya, dressed up as butterflies of various colours. You could hear the music; it would take you along with it. The music was so loud that you could hear it from a far distance. People of all ages, young and old, were there. For four days and nights, the festival continued.

From among the crowd, Jonathan stood and spotted her immediately from a far distance, full of life and energy. He stood on the spot as if paralyzed; he could not take his eyes off her as she gracefully danced among the crowds. He could not resist her innocence . . . It was not her beauty that attracted him, though. He came across many beautiful women. He was admiring her spirit that lured him. She was different from any other woman he had met; he was aware of that. Jonathan was lost for words. He was falling crazily in love with her. He was the kind of love-'em-and-leave-'em person. He was rich, dashing, and had everything, but he could not do that to her. He wanted desperately to talk to her; he jumped into the crowd and bumped into her. "You're here!" he said with a smile. "I was afraid that somebody might prevent you from talking to me. You look beautiful with or without your costume," he said. "So beautiful that when I see you, it is as if you are not for real."

They moved through the ever-increasing crowd, stopping here and there to chat.

"But I'm real!" Sheena smiled, still walking in the crowd. "Why are you staring at me like that? You're making me feel embarrassed," she said.

Jonathan was staring at her intensively. He could not take his eyes off her. Eventually, he realized he was staring. Her voice was soft and gentle. "Forgive me! I didn't mean to be rude. Please forgive me," Jonathan said as she moved past him, and he caught a faint scent of her perfume, something light and floral on her skin.

"Please slow down. I like to talk to you. I haven't properly introduced myself. My name is Jonathan Samson," he announced. "There are a lot of things I want to say to you which would be impossible with a crowd of people and music."

She stopped for a moment and shook her head, smiling. "I'm sorry, I can't. Don't you have something better to do than stare?"

"Nope," he responded, smiling.

Sheena increased her pace, dancing among the floats. Disappointment surged through him. Jonathan hurried after her.

"Well, look in another direction."

"I want to see you. If I'm not depriving you, how about tomorrow?" He grinned.

"No!"

"Please!" he pleaded.

"No!"

"Go on, please!"

"Okay." She nodded and smiled. "I'll be going to the market with my grandma. I will meet you halfway early morning."

"Okay. How, about three-thirty?"

"Okay."

"So I'll see you tomorrow," he said firmly. "Goodbye, Sheena."

"Bye." She smiled.

He walked away, feeling light and happy. He could not wait to see her again.

The next day, Sheena woke up early, far earlier than she usually did, and decided it was impossible to stay in bed. She put on her colourful sleeveless dress that was hanging in the wardrobe. The sun was shining, and the birds were singing outside her window. She had her breakfast, fried bananas, and went out into the garden. Everyone was up. Sheena's mother was outside in the yard, feeding the hogs and chicken before she set out to work. It was another beautiful day. She went up to her father, telling him that she will be going into town on an errand. Datilda asked her to go with her to the market. Her eyes widened as she gave Sheena a smile and a wink, but Leon did not notice. The recognition on her face was enough for Sheena; the look on her face said it all. "Are you ready with your plan?"

She responded, "Yes!" As they were leaving, Leon approached his mother and told her to keep an eye on her. Sheena felt as if she was spied on even by her grandma. As they were driving along the road under the heat, Datilda began to say something, "Sheena!"

"Yes, Grandma," responded Sheena.

"If you like the young man, why won't you see him?" Datilda asked.

Sheena was surprised to hear these words coming from her; she was wondering.

"Don't worry, I too was young!" said Datilda. "Sometimes I don't like the way my son treats you. He's too hard on you . . . He's a nice young man," continued Datilda.

Sheena then replied, "I will see him before we reach the market."

"Good!" said Datilda.

Jonathan pulled out of his garage and headed out to the country. He thought what a glorious morning it was, the kind of day that made him feel good to be alive. Opening the window of the jeep, he took a few deep breaths of the pure clean air. Jonathan was feeling better in spirits after his meeting with Sheena. He was very much drawn to her just as he had been the day before, but this time, the feeling was more powerful.

On their way to town, on both sides of the road were children of all ages released from school, wearing their school uniforms with matching ribbons on girls' braids, most carrying their books in their hands or in plastic bags. Only the boys had their shirts hanging out, shoelaces untied, and elderly people were passing by. As they continued driving before they reached the town, they could see a jeep approaching them in the opposite direction. It was Jonathan. He stopped and waited in the road until their car was near. When they met, the first thing Jonathan noticed about her was her exciting exotic look. He looked at Datilda and greeted her with a smile. Sheena eased Jonathan by telling him that with her their secret was safe.

"She's okay! She's not like my father. She won't say a word."

"Okay!" said Jonathan.

Jonathan reversed his jeep and swung it around before following them halfway along the road before turning off into another road. Datilda turned round toward the window of the car and began to say, "Take care of her, and bring her back for five o'clock here. In this way, no one will suspect anything."

"I will do!" replied Jonathan with a smile, holding Sheena's hand.

A delicious smell came suddenly drifting out in the air. He inhaled then sniffed. Datilda turned around and said, "I baked these earlier this morning, and they are still warm. Would you like one? It's delicious."

"No, no, I can manage."

Sheena left her grandma and went off with Jonathan in his jeep and set off along the road, leaving her on her way to town. As they arrived, Jonathan stopped his jeep near the natural pool, where there was a magnificent waterfall. Sheena was so happy. At first, she did not know who he really was. She wondered if he had a girlfriend. Obviously, he did, she thought, looking the way he looked. It was more likely that women chased after him. Of course, he had never been interested in her, so why daydream about him? Which is exactly what she had done since their first meeting. Actually, she could not get him out of her mind.

"Let's go swimming," Jonathan said, looking at her.

She got up from where she was sitting, pulled her dress over her head, revealing a colourful bikini top and shorts underneath. He stared at her, unable to take his eyes from the perfect skin, taking in every curve of her sculptured body. When his eyes finally met hers, she smiled. He took off his T-shirt, leaving his shorts. "Come on," he said. She felt uncomfortable and feeling unsure of herself. Jonathan went down to the water's edge, pulling her in the water. He went further into the water and went under and stood up from the water, shaking his head with water dripping from his face and back. She splashed more water on his face and began to run. She looked back to see him coming after her.

"I'm sorry! I'm sorry!" she laughed and screamed as he came closer. "Jonathan, I'm sorry!" As she swam toward the waterfall, they stopped. He moved toward her. Her heart flipped. He was close enough to grab her. They stood there, looking at each other for a moment, smiling while the water was pouring over her. He held her close; she struggled to be free. He looked at her, looked right into her eyes, and he felt the hairs on the back of his neck bristling. There was something about her. She was different. He was drawn to her.

"What are you thinking about?" Sheena asked in a soft voice.

"I want to tell you something . . . but I'm not sure how to tell you."

"What is it?" she asked, feeling worried. "Just say it."

The touch of his hand on hers electrified her whole body. She felt her heart pumped out of her chest. Jonathan moved slowly toward Sheena. He stroked her hair and tried to kiss her.

"No!" she said, pulling away.

"Why?" asked Jonathan.

"I know it would be a mistake," responded Sheena.

"A mistake for whom?" Jonathan asked. "How can you say such a thing? It is not a mistake where I am concerned." He said, looking directly at her, "This is not a game for me. I feel that you should know . . . that . . . I . . . I've liked you ever since the day we first met."

"Really?" she asked in disbelief.

"Yes, Sheena, you make me feel alive," he said, looking deep into her eyes. Again, he tried to kiss her, but Sheena moved one step back.

"You are so beautiful," he whispered. "I love you, it's true!" said Jonathan, gazing down at her under the water that was pouring on her face from the falls. "I should not have told you that. I just want you to know that I'm serious about you."

"Seriously, I don't think you know the meaning of serious. You think you're falling in love. You have a reputation of being a playboy. You might change your mind," she said.

"I've never been surer of anything in my entire life till now."

Moving closer to her, he put his arms around her and held her against him. He knew she was the woman for him, the only woman he wanted. For a moment, she could not speak. This was not happening . . . this was not real. Jonathan drew close and gently stroked her hair. Again he could not help himself, he bent down and kissed her fully on her mouth. She kissed him back, pressing her body against his because she was tall, almost as tall as he was. Their bodies fitted together. They were alone together at last.

After a few minutes of intense kissing, they stopped, drew apart, and stared at each other breathlessly. Jonathan said softly, "I've been waiting to do that for a long time." The more they got to know each other, the more their feeling grew. They swam and played in the water like little children. He grabbed her around the middle and lifted her up. She screamed as she plunged head first into the water. He swam away, and she gave chase grabbing his legs, and tried ducking him as they splashed and laughed until it was time to go back, keeping his word with Datilda. While they were getting dressed, Jonathan began to ask, "Tell me something about you?"

"Well, I'm a good girl." She laughed.

"Are you going to university?"

"Yes, but . . . family reasons."

"You're very beautiful."

"What's beautiful about me?"

"Everything." He laughed. "You have really pretty eyes, and when you smile, your whole face lights up."

"Keep going."

"I actually think you're the most beautiful girl I've ever met."

"I'll copy your remarks into my diary tonight."

"Do you keep a diary?"

"Yes, I do. It is simply a girl's record of her own thoughts and impressions."

"What do you like about me?" Jonathan asked.

"Umm . . . I don't know . . . ," she said, looking at him. "You're strong, sensitive, and I like your face and eyes. You smile a lot."

He looked at her and smiled as they were walking back to the jeep. They entered his jeep and drove. As they arrived at the meeting point, Datilda was not there. Sheena was worried that something might have happened to her, but at a very far distance, Jonathan could see her car. It was moving very slowly; she had a flat tire. Jonathan joined her with his jeep and asked to take them both home, leaving the car behind. Sheena replied, "No!"

She was afraid of the reaction of her father, but Datilda responded, "Yes!"

"Grandma, what will Father say if he sees us in the jeep?" asked Sheena worriedly.

"Nothing! If I am with you, he can't say anything," responded Datilda.

He opened the back passenger door on the far side. "Get in." He helped Datilda into his jeep and told Sheena to sit at the back with her and drove off.

Suddenly, Rusty raised and tilted his head to the side and barked as a vehicle approached. Everyone turned and looked and saw a jeep arriving; they did not know who it was until they saw who was behind the wheel. Jonathan slowed down to avoid hitting him. He parked his jeep just outside Sheena's house, stepped out, and opened the door for Datilda. She was not able to come out, being high from the ground and being a very old woman. He gave her his hands, and she took them. As she stepped out, she lost her balance a bit. He moved closer to prevent her from stumbling.

He held her for a moment; she thanked him and walked off with Sheena toward the house to rest. Glenn walked up.

"Hey, man, how's things?"

"Fine," he replied with a smile.

"Let's talk about getting overworked and burned out." Glenn continued to talk with Jonathan about extra work at the company.

During dinner, sitting at the dinner table with the whole family, Leon would look at his daughter now and then. He was quiet and did not finish his food. Everyone knew him; he wasn't one to pass on good food. After everyone had finished eating, Leon decided to go sit outside on the terrace. Meanwhile, Datilda noticed that her son was troubled about something, so she followed him on the terrace too. Her son turned around and saw his mother. He told her to sit next to him on the swing seat suspended from the iron framework. She sat next to him and placed her hands on his lap, giving him a sense of comfort. The rest of the family was inside, helping their mother clean up. Datilda saw that her son was in deep thoughts on something that she asked what was on his mind.

"You're quiet. What's upsetting you?" asked Datilda.

"What do you mean?" asked Leon.

"Is something bothering you?" Datilda asked.

Leon ignored the question and was silent for a moment then a reply came, "No! It's not true . . . Why you ask?"

"Because that's what mothers do, we ask, we care, and we worry . . . It is Sheena, isn't it? Ah!" said Datilda.

"What must I do?" asked Leon, shaking his head.

"Nothing!" answered Datilda. "What is there to do?"

Being father and husband of the family, it was not easy to accept that Sheena, the baby of the family, was growing up, and he was afraid that one day she would drift away, and maybe they would never see her again. This was very hard for him. All the rest of the family were either married, engaged to be married, or at school because they were too young. All were one way or another, involved with someone except for Sheena. Back inside the house, Drusilla walked up to Sheena to talk to her in private.

"Sis, I'm not saying anything to you, but just be careful what you do with yourself."

"What do you mean by that?"

"Nothing, just that I'm your older sister and, having more experience than you, I can only say that, over the years, I've discovered that the more you love a person, the more they're bound to disappoint you in the end! Do you know him?" she asked wondering.

"No, not well enough."

"Just be careful. He'll be after you, like the others," she continued.

During the first night, when she went to bed, Sheena was unable to sleep well. She was woken by the fact that she had dreamt about Jonathan. Everywhere was dark and very quiet. Reaching out, she turned on the bedside lamp and looked at the clock. It was four fifteen. She roused from her bed, thinking about Jonathan. She was falling in love with him. She should not, but she was, and she did not know how to stop herself. Leon was not able to sleep that night too; his mind was troubled.

31

He sat up for a while and then got out of bed and went to Sheena's room. It had just stopped raining. He knocked and opened the door. She was still awake. As her father entered the room, she quickly folded the letter and placed it in between the pages of her book that was on the table and placed the book in the drawer without her father suspecting anything. Sheena looked at her father and noticed the expression on his face. He was sad.

"What's wrong?"

"I can't sleep," responded Leon.

"Why?" she asked.

"I just wanted to know how you feel, that's all," he said.

"Feel about what?" asked Sheena, confused.

"About leaving the family, getting married, or to live abroad, you know."

"Father, I know you want to talk, but can we talk about it in the morning. It's late. It's four forty-five in the morning," she said.

"Yes, you're right. It's late," he said.

He could not go to sleep without asking, so he began to ask her question to see what she thought about leaving the island and living in another country without the family.

"Do we have to talk about this now?"

She did not answer because she knew very well how her father felt about the idea. It was better to avoid any displeasure between the two and repeated that it was late and slid down under the covers and attempted to go back to sleep. Jonathan too, that same night, could not sleep; his mind was filled with thoughts of Sheena. They had only known each other only five weeks, yet it seemed so much longer. He had discovered that they liked the same things. She had a good sense of humor, laughed a lot, and had talent. She was not hard.

"Am I falling in love?" he asked himself. "I've never felt this way before. It can't be love. I hardly even know her. I know I told her I love her, but I can't believe that I am. You don't fall in love this easily," he said to himself.

It was Sunday morning; the sun was seeping through the gaps in the curtains. The family was preparing for their Sunday service. As the family arrived at the congregation, Leon saw Jonathan there too. Sheena pretended that she did not see him and walked past him toward the entrance of the church. She overheard that he was leaving for Seattle in the morning. The look on Sheena's face changed. During the service, Sheena would have a quick glimpse at Jonathan. There was a very strong feeling between the two. After the service had ended, the minister of the church went over to Jonathan and Grace to thank them. Leon approached the minister and asked if he knew them. Datilda walked up to her son and told him that she wanted to go and visit her husband alone, who had died six years ago. She arrived at his tomb and sat down next to it and began to talk to him.

"Well, Gilbert, here I am. I'm getting very old now. I can feel it in my bones too. I will be joining you soon, but I hope when everything is okay in the family, that will be my time to leave." then she continued, "Your son, Leon, the older he gets, the more trouble he gives than when he was a child. There's a young man. His name's Jonathan, and he is the son of err . . . the Samson. He's good. Let's hope God give me more strength before I die that Sheena marries this young man. You know what I went through with them." She got up and passed her hands over Gilbert's picture on the tombstone and said her farewells and headed off toward the family that were still there outside the building, talking to their minister.

Leon saw his mother approaching and told the family it was time to leave, and they said their goodbyes to the minister. After they all returned home and had dinner, Eric, a friend of the family, who moved away from the village into the city, passed by to greet them. Everyone greeted him with surprise. Datilda walked over to him and held his face in her hands. "He's all grown up now . . . I remember when you were a small boy."

Eric smiled. "I know." Leon, with a long smile on his face, was happy to see him. He walked over and places his hands on his back. Sheena looked up to Eric and greeted him too. Eric has always been in love with her. Trouble is, Sheena only ever wanted to be friends.

"Eric, man, what took you so long to come and see us?" asked Leon, embracing him with a smile.

"Hey, Sheena, it's good to see you. You've grown up into a beautiful woman too," he said, smiling.

"It's good to see you too. How are things going with you in the big city, Eric?"

"Fine." with a smile on his face.

"Sheena, I came by because soon you will be having your driving test, and I want to do something special for you," said Eric.

"You don't have to . . . ," said Sheena.

"I want to!" insisted Eric.

"It's no big deal. You're my best friend. I would do anything for you," said Eric.

Sheena smiled up at him, and Eric smiled back. Ever since they'd been twelve, he had always been the one to look after her. She was like a sister. Eric remained with the family, telling them what the city life was like and that he had been to America. Sheena was fascinated by the stories that Eric told. Glenn roused from his seat and left the house to go into town. While hanging out with his friends, he saw Jonathan sitting outside a wine bar with some friends. Glenn went up to Jonathan to greet him.

"Hi, Jonathan. You're back!"

"Hi, Glenn. Yes!"

Jonathan roused from his seat and told Glenn to follow him, leaving his friend at the table. His friends looked at each other, wondering what relationship Jonathan had with Glenn. Following him, leaving his friends behind, Jonathan said, "I need you to do me a favour. I need you to give this note to your sister, Sheena." Glenn took the note and placed it in his pocket, and they both went back to their friends.

As the evening was ending back at the Beckers, Sheena asked Jalissa, after she managed eventually to get her grief of a heartbroken relationship under control, to start another relationship, being there had been several men interested in her. Jalissa shook her head and said, "I haven't found the right one. I'm looking to fall head over heels in love. I want my stomach to lurch and my knees to wobble," She laughed and continued, "I want to be swept off my feet into his arms. It must be like that for me."

"Yeah, yeah," Cattleya said in a sarcastic way. "Keep on dreaming."

"Well, we're off, Sheena. You must be very tired," said Cattleya. "See you later."

As soon as Glenn returned home that evening, he knocked on Sheena's room and told her in secret that he had a note from Jonathan. He handed her the note. She looked at Glenn worried, but he eased her by telling her that their secret was safe with him and warned her to safely burn the letter when she finished reading it. She waited to be alone and began to read.

Sheena,

I always dreamt of finding the woman of my life. From the moment you came into my life, I knew that our friendship would turn into something lasting. You make me feel more like myself ALIVE where no other woman has inspired me this way. You brought me back to life. You've brightened my world with the warmth of your presence, and you're my light in the dark.

Jonathan

CHAPTER FOUR

*I*t was very late. Leon decided before going to bed to say good night to his daughter. He knocked on her door. While he was entering, Sheena was putting away the letter before he could see it.

"Did I wake you?"

"No."

Before he left the room, he smiled and asked her what she was reading when he came in the room. Sheena denied that she was reading something. Leon insisted and asked to see it, thinking that it was a letter from Eric, her childhood friend, knowing that Eric was fond of her. She opened the drawer and took out the book where she had placed the note and gave it to her father. He opened the note and began to read it. His face changed from a smile to anger. He stared at her, a small frown knotting his brow. He shook his head with this pleasure then tore the note in half and threw it away, forbidding her to see him.

"Forget all about him and his family. Don't see him again!" ordered her father. Eric Sanchez is an honest young man . . . You don't need this Jonathan Samson!" continued Leon. These words were so hard that she turned her back to her father and faced the window and began to weep. He closed the door and went to his room. Coretta saw Leon enter the room, wondering why he wasn't in bed and why all the shouting. She noticed the expression on his face and asked what was wrong.

"I can't believe that Sheena, all this time, has been seeing the Samsons' son!" he said angrily.

"I think he is a good young man," responded Coretta.

"He's a Samson! You know what the Samson did to my family!" responded Leon with a livid voice.

"Honey, I know! I know! . . . I'll talk to Sheena. Now go to sleep," said Coretta sighing.

Coretta covered the both of them and tucked herself close to his side.

"Good night," Coretta whispered drowsily.

"Good night," respond Leon.

He listened to her breathing, he realize she had gone to sleep. Smiling to himself he turned to kiss her a good night on her forehead.

It was morning; everyone was out except for Sheena's father. Leon knocked on the bedroom door. In his hand he had a small red box. As he entered the room, Sheena sat up on her bed with a sad smile on her face. Her father smiled as if nothing happened and happily said, handing over a small box, "You've done it, you've got your license! This is a gift from the entire family. I found a really cheap gift for you," he said. Sheena looked at the box, wondering.

"What kind of present?"

"Well, honey, I've already bought it as a gift."

"How cheap is it?"

"Well, have a look inside the box."

She opened it. Her eyes lit with joy. It was what she always wanted—a car. She jumped from her bed and hugged her father. She ran over to the window, looked out, and responded, "That's really nice, Paps. Thanks!"

"I don't mind. I want you to be happy."

"Now I wouldn't be fazed to use your horrific car again." Sheena smiled, teasing her father.

"It's my car."

The following evening, her mother came in the room with a smile on her face while she was getting ready. She approached Sheena and helped her to do her hair. "Child, Eric is a good man. You've known him since childhood. Don't you find him handsome-looking?" she asked "When I married your father, I was happy. Are you listening to me?" Coretta said, quickly glancing at her.

"Mama, please."

"Have you never thought of being with him?"

"Why?"

"I'm just asking, that's all."

She shook her head. "Eric is handsome, but he's just my good friend," Sheena responded.

"Only your good friend?" questioned Coretta.

"Okay, my best friend. Why?" asked Sheena. "I care about Eric. Eric's been in my life from when we were kids. We're good friends, and we have a lot in common. He's always encouraged me in my studies, never stood away whenever I needed him. He's a nice guy."

"Listen, Sheena, I have not told you this before. Being there was no point, but you must promise me that you will not see him again . . . It's better."

"Who? Why not?" Sheena asked.

"Nothing!" answered Coretta, not giving out too much information to ruin an important evening for Sheena. "It's late, and Eric will be here soon, so hurry up!" Coretta said, expressing annoyance.

Eric showed up that evening with a bunch of flowers. Coretta was smiling; she understood that he had an interest toward Sheena. Glenn, in the meantime, was not very keen on Eric, knowing his character. Thirty minutes later, Sheena walked out of her room and walked slowly down the steps.

"Oh, here she is now!" Coretta said excitedly. Eric gazed at her beauty. Sheena was no longer the long-legged girl he grew up with. She was beautiful. Eric gave the flowers to Sheena.

"Thank you, Eric!" She smiled up at him. "You didn't have to," said Sheena. As they were walking out through the door, they said their goodbyes and walked toward the car. Eric took Sheena's hands and said, "You look really pretty, by the way."

"Um, thanks," responded Sheena.

As they entered his polished black Fiat Spider 124, Sheena looked through the window at her parents and waved while the car was moving. As they were approaching the town to where Eric had arranged a special surprise, Sheena was thinking about Jonathan. The car stopped to a point; Eric came out of the car and opened the door. Sheena stepped out and walked along side him. He asked Sheena to close her eyes. She closed her eyes, wondering at the same time what he had planned for her. He guided her while they walked up to a point, then they stopped. Sheena opened her eyes and saw a building that was surprisingly lighted up with lights along with colourful ribbons with her name on them. As they entered the restaurant, Sheena's face was happy.

"Eric! What's all this?" she asked.

"It's a surprise," replied Eric. "I booked us a table here."

"Eric . . . it's so beautiful. Thank you!"

"You're my best friend. This is a surprise gift, and I had to give something special to a special friend. Congratulations, Sheena!" said Eric joyfully.

"For what?"

"Your father told me that you passed your driving test."

She looked at the restaurant that Eric had picked. It was small and intimate. The door of the premises opened, and they entered. The restaurant seemed overcrowded; she smiled in a friendly way to Eric as the waitress accompanied them to a table. There was jazz in the background. She could see everyone was looking at her from the corner of their eyes as she walked across the room. Every eye in the room seems to be on her. The men were obviously looking at her because she was just simply beautiful, and the women were envious. The waitress approached them and escorted them to one of the best tables with a menu.

"Can I bring you something to drink?"

"Yes, two glasses of wine, please, Bellini's, and water."

Once the waitress had taken their order, they were alone. Sheena said, "How is your business going in the city?"

"Good," he explained.

"I know you like doing windsurfing, and you're pretty good at it too."

"Thanks. And you?"

Before she could answer, the waitress was back placing the appetizers in front of them. It all looked delicious.

"Thank you!"

"Not much," she answered.

They ate and talked all night. As the evening was coming to its end. Eric plucked up enough courage and asked if Sheena wanted to join him to dance. She was a bit embarrassed.

"No, I'm not in the mood."

Eric got up from the table, taking her by the hand. He pulled her to the dance floor, giving her a little spin before he took her into his arms. He placed his hand around her waist, and hers were on his shoulders, and they moved to the music that had slow rhythm all night. Finally, he asked, "Do you want to go outside for a bit?" She nodded as he took her by the hand, again, leading her outside where there were tables and guests sitting. While the evening was coming to an end, there was a breeze blowing. It was starting to get a bit cold. Sheena felt a draft.

"You're cold. I'm a bit cold myself," Eric admitted.

"I'll be okay . . . I should have brought with me my shawl. It's my fault."

"Here," he said, "wrap this around you." Eric handed her his jacket. "Let's go back. It's warmer inside."

"Oh, Eric, thank you," responded Sheena.

Once inside, Sheena looked at her watch. She said, "It's getting very late, I think it's better if we start making our way back."

"Yes, you're right."

She stood outside the restaurant after their dinner, while Eric went to fetch the car. He opened the door for her to enter and took her home. That same evening, Jonathan rang Glenn.

"I need to see you, right away."

"Where do you want to meet?"

"Anywhere."

"Meet me in town."

Half an hour later, Glenn saw Jonathan sitting at a table alone outside a pub.

"What's wrong?"

Jonathan wondered if he could persuade Glenn to help him make Sheena slip away from the house. He took a deep breath.

"Glenn, could you to do me a favour? But please don't ask questions. I want you to help me."

"You're in love with my sister, aren't you?"

Jonathan replied, "Err . . . thanks again. I owe you one."

"That's what friends are for. Maybe one day I will need you for something," said Glenn.

CHAPTER FIVE

*I*t was almost midnight when Glenn pulled into the driveway. He entered the house and went into Sheena's room. Sheena was in her room, lying silently on her stomach on the bed, with the door slightly opened. Glenn enters the room and gave her a note, and she began to read.

> *Sheena, I must see you tonight. Meet me at 1:00 a.m.*
> *I will be waiting near the mango tree.*

> *Jonathan*

Jonathan knew there would be a full moon that night; he chose the spot not far from the lake to prepare the surprise. He began to see if everything was in order. "Okay, so everything is set up: candles? Check. Flowers? Check." Everything was ready. Jonathan stepped back, looking at what he had done. The candles and food were set out on a picnic blanket. The stars in the sky shone so bright like they had never shone before. Jonathan felt ready. He went in his jeep and drove off to pick Sheena up near her home with Glenn's help. Jonathan wandered near one of the trees, wondering if Sheena could slip away from the house to go with him to their secret place they both loved. Her spirit healed and inspired him. He began to find happiness and meaning in his life.

"I have to talk to her," he told himself. "I have to tell her that nothing matters except our love for each other."

It was after midnight, he glanced at his watch. Sheena was in her room. She heard her parents go to bed about an hour ago. She did not want to take any chances. She looked at her clock, got dressed, and reached for the switch of the table lamp and switched it off and lit a candle that was on her dressing table. She opened the door very quietly and tiptoed and hurried as silently as possible along the corridor and made sure not to wake her parents. She carried her shoes in one hand and a lamp in the other. She went down the stairs, guided only by a faint light into the kitchen. Glenn was in the kitchen, waiting for her. He took hold of the candle, opened the door, and held her hand, and they both ran out into the yard. Rusty was woken by Sheena and Glenn's footsteps but didn't bark. Glenn went over to put him back to sleep and told her to continue ahead without him. Sheena had not even thought of not being the same level as him, who cared if he attended an important university or if his name was printed in a business newspaper. Jonathan was waiting for her; he could see Sheena walking very quickly to where he was. He was too anxious to wait, so he rushed quickly toward her. Before she could put her shoes on or say anything, Jonathan grabbed her and kissed her passionately and demandingly. "You came!" he said, smiling.

"I couldn't sleep, I had to see you." He stretched out his hand and guided her toward his jeep. "Come, I want to tell you something."

Her common sense told her not to get involved with him, but the touch of his hands and the way he made her feel were too much to resist. He pulled her close into his arms he felt her body close to his; she felt his heart pounding against her chest. One hand held the back of her head, holding her still, while the other stroked her hair. He leaned toward her, only inches separated their lips. There was no need for words. She met his gaze then lightly brushed her lips against his. He kissed her until he took her heart between her lips and made it his. She melted against his chest and poured everything passionate within her into the kiss. They walked for a few seconds until they arrived at the spot. They sat down where Jonathan had laid everything, but one, before he left her to get the one thing that was missing, he asked a question, "Did you tell your father about us?"

She smiled and said, "No, I didn't. The fact that you didn't even think that it's possible that you can keep something like this from your own family"—she looked into his eyes—"it's just further proof that you're not ready!" he looked at her. "Your father doesn't know about us, does he?" asked Sheena.

"No, no! But I don't see why it should be a problem," responded Jonathan smiling.

"Let's say, if he knew?"

"It would be like a red flag to a bull. I don't care if he knew, you know. I'm a big boy. I can look after myself."

He got up and walked over to his jeep. He took a large black box with a red rose attached to it out from the backseat of his jeep and walked back and handed the box over to her. Sheena smiled while taking the box.

"This is for you."

"What is it?" Sheena asked.

"You'll like it, open it."

Jonathan sat down next to her and watched her open the box. She lifted the cover and saw a beautiful blue silk dress. She was all smiles, overjoyed with the dress in her hands.

"Thank you. It's beautiful."

"You're welcome. I hope it's beautiful enough for you."

Jonathan took Sheena, and they held hand in hand by the lake under the light of the full moon. He put his hand around her and hugged her. "I'm glad we met, and I'm glad you came." He stopped and looked at her, a faint smile briefly touched his mouth. "Whatever your circumstances are, Sheena, you're the best thing that's happened to me in a long time." He kissed the tip of her nose.

She nodded. "Me too." She threw her arms around his neck, pulled his face close to hers.

"Sheena."

"What?"

"I still think you're beautiful."

"What else?"

"Your smile, when I catch one, it shines like the sun."

"Oh."

"Now what?" he asked.

"I want you to look at me as if I am the only woman in this world."

"I've been doing that since the first moment I saw you." She smiled and sealed it with a kiss.

"I have to go home now. I don't want my father to suspect something."

They left the things lying on the ground and walked toward the jeep. He drove her as far as where they met.

"Let's do something nice tomorrow. Wear the dress. We can go to a very nice restaurant or a nightclub . . . Whatever you like."

"I'll see you tomorrow around this time near the mango tree."

"I'll be waiting." Jonathan smiled.

"Call me when everything is safe, when you get in."

"I will," Sheena replied.

A few hours later, back at the Samson mansion, Grace and Steven were in the lounge in front of the fireplace, drinking wine. The front entrance of the house opened. Jonathan entered, placing his car keys on a side table in the hallway. Walking silently past the lounge, he heard his mother's voice call him.

"Jonathan, dear," Grace said.

"Yes, Mother."

"Come sit with us."

"No, Mother, I'm a little tired tonight."

"Okay, good night, dear."

As he walked halfway up the steps to his room, his phone rang. Sheena was on the other side. Smiling happily, he flipped it open to answer.

"Hi!"

"Hi! Teeth brushed and ready for bed," she said, smiling.

"Good. I'm glad."

"Is everything all right? You sound serious," Sheena asked.

"No, no, few minutes left to normal. I'll see you tomorrow."

"I had a really nice time this evening on our date."

"You're such a liar," said Jonathan sarcastically.

"No, I'm serious. In a way, it was exactly as I thought it would be."

"I had a really nice time too," said Jonathan.

Whenever it was possible without any suspicion, they met. Steven Samson was arriving from Seattle after concluding a business deal. News got around at the company that Steven Samson was leaving America for the island; all the workers were not very happy. He was not polite or kind to anyone who was working for him. He arrived at the airport and was taken directly to the company. He entered the building without saying a word to anyone; all his personal staff was looking at him no smile, no greetings. As he walked past his assistant's desk, she greeted him with a smile.

"Welcome back, Mr. Samson."

"Anything that needs attending to before the ten o'clock meeting?" asked Steven.

She smiled prettily and shook her bleached-blond hair.

"Nothing that won't keep."

"Great," he answered. "Oh, if I get a call from my wife, I want to take it. Besides that, I don't want to be interrupted."

"Certainly," she responded.

"Are there any messages for me?" Steven asked.

"No, Mr. Samson, no messages, no, nothing at all."

"Thank you."

He turned and walked straight into his large office, throwing his jacket on the sofa and placing his briefcase on his desk, sat down, looked at his appointment book, stared at the dates, and called his secretary for a coffee. Shelia knocked on the door, entered the office, holding in one hand a strong, rich coffee perfuming the air. She left the coffee on the corner of his desk.

"Thanks, Shelia. How do I look?"

"You look very tired."

She approached him with letters and said, "There are some letters. It's nothing urgent. I'll leave the letters here to sign."

"Okay."

He lit himself a cigar and sat down on his chair when, a few moments later, he had an unexpected call. The phone rang; Shelia left the office quickly, closing the door behind her. By ten o'clock, Steven was in a conference with a number of business people when his secretary buzzed.

"Excuse me, Mr. Samson. There's a call for you."

"Shelia, I told you no interruptions."

"It's urgent, and it's on line two."

Steven turned to his guests and said. "We'll finish this later, gentlemen. If you'll excuse me."

He watched them leave his room, and when the door closed behind them, he picked up the phone.

"Hello."

"Hello," answered the voice on the other side. "Are you Steven Samson?" the voice asked.

"Yes, I am. It's me speaking. What can I do for you?" Steven asked.

"Well, I have some news for you about your son," said the voice.

"My son?" said Steven worried. "What's wrong with my son?" asked Steven.

"You have no idea what's being going on while you were away on business . . . do you? Your son has a sort of a love story with a country girl on the island," responded the voice on the phone.

"W-What do you mean a love story?" shouted Steven. "Who are you?" he questioned.

He set the phone back down in its cradle on his desk angrily and, extremely upset, stubbed his cigar out in the ashtray and left it there and decided to leave his office and went home to his wife, Grace. Steven was too agitated due to the unexpected call. The Samsons' house was large; the front door opened onto a carpeted entryway. A wide doorway on the right led to the den, and straight ahead was a long hallway to the kitchen on the left. The stairs went up to a landing that overlooked the foyer. Grace and Jonathan were at home. Grace heard a car parked outside the house; it was her husband. Steven opened the door and entered the house and shouted with a loud voice down the hallway to Charlotte, his maid, "Is there brandy?"

"Yes, Mr. Steven."

Steven waved his hand. "Tell my wife that I am here." He slammed the door behind him in a forceful manner and headed straight to the studio. He poured himself a glass of brandy and slumped into his favourite armchair. He took a long sip and gazed at the fireplace. He was tired. He stretched out his legs and leaned his head back with his eyes closed. Grace entered the room and froze. She looked at him.

"This is a surprise," said Grace, surprisingly, walking forward. "You're home early, I wasn't expecting you so early."

He rose from his seat, nodded, and kissed her on the cheek as she drew to a standstill. "Yes. Where in the blazes is Jonathan?" he said fiercely.

Grace was worried and called out to her son, "Jonathan! Jonathan! Your father's here. He wants to talk to you."

"What's wrong?" asked Grace worried. "Something's happened?"

"Yes!" responded Steven angrily, placing his jacket on the chair.

Steven entered his studio and asked Grace to send Jonathan to him. Jonathan came down and asked his mother why his father wanted to see him. Jonathan entered the studio, where he found his father standing firm. He closed the door behind him, and they began to talk. Grace, in the meantime, was in the lounge when she heard two hushed voices turn into a raging battle of disagreement.

Both were shouting at each other. Their yelling became so extreme that Grace entered the room. Jonathan was very angry.

"Calm down the both of you!" Grace said. "What's the matter, dear?" Grace asked her husband.

"It's our son," responded Steven.

"What has he done?" asked Grace, worried.

"You don't know?" responded Steven, still yelling. "The entire damn town is talking about it!"

"About what, dear?" asked Grace surprised.

"I return on this island to receive a call from someone telling me that OUR son—yes, our son—is in love with . . . with . . . with . . ."

"Oh yes, it's true!" Grace confirmed what the rumours were about.

"You knew, and you allowed our son? This is outrageous!" responded Steven angrily.

"What could I do? He's our son," responded Grace.

"What could you have done? I'll tell you what you could have done!" responded Steven outrageously.

Jonathan interrupted their discussion, telling them that he was old enough to be in love and was old enough to decide for himself who he wanted. He wanted to get away from the screams of his father into his ears. Grace turned around to her son.

"You are not to think about yourself, but for the family and our reputation too!"

Suddenly, he glanced at his watch; he saw it was late for an appointment which he had with Sheena. Jonathan wanted so badly to leave that he stopped his mother talking, "No!" he yelled. "I can't take this, still arguing with you both . . . When I finish university, I'm going to leave you both and ask her to marry me whether you like it or not," said Jonathan.

Grace spoke, "Jonathan! Where are you going?" Before she could continue, he hurried from the room, leaving them in the studio alone, slamming the door behind him; and before you knew, it he was already out the front door.

"There," Steven triumphantly stated. "That boy will never leave. He hasn't got the guts to leave."

"No!" Grace responded. "This is wrong. You're pushing him away."

"Remember, I didn't force him to leave. It was his decision. Besides, he'll be back."

Steven felt so tired after a long flight that he told his wife that he was going to rest and that they would continue talking about the matter. Inside a wine bar, Sheena was waiting. Her anxiety was growing by the minute; there was still no sign of him. She was about to call him when she heard a car draw up outside. She saw it was Jonathan. She felt weak with relief. He walked toward her as she walked out the building. He took hold of her arms.

"I'm sorry," he said, "I was delayed. There was a lot of traffic going to the center."

"It's all right . . . I thought something had happened to you."

"Nothing's going to happen to me. Let's go in," he said, taking her hand.

During that same night, Steven could not sleep. He was restless, staring at the ceiling, thinking that there must be a way to stop the relationship. Grace woke up seeing her husband sitting in an armchair with his hands in his hair.

"Darling!" cried out Grace. "Please come back to bed."

"I can't believe our son . . . It's an embarrassment to the family!" Steven clenched his fist so tight. "After all that I've done!" exclaimed Steven.

His voice was filled with pride. "If you look at the Samsons' family tree, you will find the wife of every Samson has been of the same social standing as himself."

"I know. Let's put it this way," said Grace, "maybe it's just a crush because you know as well as I do, there is no future between the two."

Grace could not convince him because she knew that her husband was right.

"I hope you're right! Otherwise, we have to come up with something to avoid him doing something stupid. Our company is in his hands. I have no idea how we are going to deal with this. If she is scheming and clever enough, she might persuade him to marry her . . . You know as well as I do that the Samsons may have many faults, but they have never defamed our lineage!"

"But there have been a few scandals as we well know, your grandfather."

"Yes, but he didn't marry her, I know."

"That is why I exactly won't allow my son make a fool of himself and shame the family name."

Breakfast was served early the next morning, over an orange juice, scrambled eggs, toast, and bacon. Jonathan was out on the terrace, where he had a panoramic view of his garden separated from the lawn.

"Morning, Mother."

"Morning, dear. I'll have egg and one piece of bacon . . . Oh, and a coffee please, Charlotte." "Very well, madam," responded Charlotte.

Grace sat down at the table while Charlotte placed before her a plate on which was an egg and a piece of bacon.

"Morning, Father."

Charlotte returned again with two coffees and Steven's newspaper.

"Morning!" Steven responded as he sat down opposite him then flipping his newspaper back up. "Where were you last night?" he said, speaking with a newspaper held in front of him like a barrier between them.

"You didn't get home until four o'clock in the morning," Grace said.

"You shouldn't have waited up for me. I told you not to," Jonathan answered imprudently. His father voice was fierce. He lowered the newspaper. "Don't you dare raise or answer me back in that tone of voice, young man. Who do you think you are?"

Jonathan was so angry that he shook his head, and he immediately rose from the table, throwing the napkin on the table as he said, "I don't think I should be here to hear you tell me what I should or shouldn't do with my life. I've grown up now. Maybe you haven't noticed that, or you just can't see for how busy you are in your work! I'll take care of my own life, okay? Think that's clear enough?" he continued.

"No, you're wrong, Jonathan," Steven said, raising his voice.

Grace yelled after him, "Jonathan!" While the maid was entering the room onto the terrace, she overheard the discussion between Jonathan and his father. Steven turned around just before he was about to take the glass of orange juice from the tray. He insulted Sheena, by pointing his finger at his maid. "She's a PEASANT! Who serves like everyone else here like her and not only, she's a N! and nothing else. What can you get from nothing? NOTHING!" he shouted.

Grace was marvelled to hear her husband react in such a way toward the maid who had served her family when her father was alive, the last Richardson, after a very long and lingering illness. Everyone had attended his funeral from the village and the congregation which was a mile drive. Steven Samson was chosen to take over the Richardson Company after the death of Joseph Murphy Richardson. He held his first business party at his house with friends. The maid felt desire to throw the full glass of squeezed orange in his face; instead, she dropped the tray with all the cutleries, took off her apron, and spat on the floor toward Steven and walked out. Grace ran toward her, trying to convince her to stay, but she refused. She did not know what to do. Jonathan in front shouted at his father, "Never use that word in reference to the woman whom I love. You haven't even met her, and you're already insulting her."

"People of the village know that you are engaged to someone else, and soon she will hear this rumour," said his father.

"That's not true! I haven't proposed marriage to anyone, and I have no intention to do so. The moment I saw her, I fell in love with her. I realized she was the one for me, and I intend to marry her with or without your consent."

"Now listen to me, boy!" Steven said furiously. "You are not going to marry her. You won't find the right woman by dating the wrong one!"

"That is exactly what I intend to do, and whatever you may say or do won't change anything!" Jonathan answered. "I am in love with her, and I'm determined to marry her, and nobody is going to stop me!"

"Over my dead body you will, boy!" shouted his father.

Jonathan spoke in such a firm manner that his father was more determined to break this scandal. He looked at Jonathan with surprise. Jonathan walked out, the front door slammed with such a fury that a rush of air entered the corridor behind him, and drove off in his jeep. Grace, entering back into the room, began to say with anger in her voice, "Charlotte is hardly a maid or servant! She's almost one of the family, having been with us for so long. She kept the house together when your father was always away on business." She continued, "When I stayed at the house for your father's funeral, I found that everything was just as it was, and that was all due to Charlotte."

"Okay! Okay! I apologize," he acknowledged. "I don't think our son should have anything to do with some country girl from this island, who would not know how to behave as a Samson!"

"I disagree with you. She can learn," pointed out Grace.

"Learn? We are not a school for farmers," Steven lectured.

Grace did not smile.

"Our son might easily be carried away by the girl who is different from those he has met in Seattle. Where are you going?"

"I've got business to take care of!" Steven exclaimed angrily.

"Don't go. We must find a way to help our son reason."

As the morning wore on, Steven walked into the lounge. He was thinking, hoping that Jonathan sees sense in what he was doing. Along the road, the maid was walking and crying. Jonathan drove near her, apologizing for his father's conduct, asking her to return back to the house. "I'm sorry! Really, I am. My father was very hard to talk to you in that manner," said Jonathan.

"You're a good person," said the maid. "Your father is too . . . too . . ."

"Let me take you home at least," begged Jonathan.

"No, I'll just walk it back," said the maid, wiping her eyes.

CHAPTER SIX

*T*hat same night, Steven told his wife Grace that their son had to go with him to the office the next day. Grace was not sure that it was a good idea, but Steven insisted he was sure about having his son around in the office. It would help to break down his new relationship. The next day, Grace did not know what to do, so she begged Jonathan to go with his father and not make things any worse than they were. Jonathan was not pleased; he was torn between two worlds. Rumor got around in the company that Steven and his son would be in the office that day.

The atmosphere was intense between the two. The office was quiet, and this disturbed Steven a lot. He called one of his staff, Joseph, who had been working for them for more than forty years, asking if he knew about the relationship of his son with one of the girls from the island. Joseph did not know what to say. He did not know whether to admit knowing or not. In the end, he told Steven that the family was decent and honest, and their daughter was called Sheena. Steven was not interested if the family was decent or honest. It was the fact that they were poor, and there was a past hidden secret. Joseph went on telling Steven that one of the family members was working for him. Steven was surprised and asked who he was. He was afraid of Steven Samson; everybody was afraid of him. Steven roused from behind his desk, walked out of his office, ordered his secretary to look for a file on Glenn Becker, and at the same time, he told Joseph to call him to his office. Joseph was worried, thinking that he would have Glenn sacked from his job. Steven shouted at Joseph, ordering him to call Glenn. In the meantime, Glenn was in his office, working away on his computer when he was interrupted by a ring tone. He picked up the receiver and answered. A voice on the other side said, "Mr. Samson would like to see you in his office."

"I'll be right there."

As he put the phone down, a strange feeling came over him. He thought a second suspiciously before he roused from his seat and headed toward the lift. There were dozens of people working at their desks in their office; they turned to stare at Glenn while he passed by.

The Samson Company was successful, fast growing with over two hundred employees. The expressions on their faces were very worrying; Glenn did not know why Steven wanted to see him. In the background, one of the lifts arrived, and people were getting out. Glenn headed for it and stepped inside and pressed the lift button and started up. When the lift reached the third floor, he stepped out and stood there for a moment, thinking before entering the secretary's office that was connected to Steven Samson's office. As he entered, he turned and looked at Shelia's face and noticed the fear in her eyes. He sat down. Shelia saw the look on his face. "Just a moment please." He nodded at her as she picked up the telephone and pressed down the intercom button.

"Mr. Samson, I'm sorry to interrupt you, Mr. Becker is here."

She listened for a moment.

"Send him in, Shelia."

She closed the intercom and turned to Glenn. "Follow me," she said.

He took a deep breath before entering Steven's office. She stopped outside Steven's office and knocked. She heard a voice behind the door shouted out, "Come in!" She opened, and they both entered the room. Shelia closed the door behind him, finding Steven on the telephone. "I'll leave it to you to arrange the details and I'll get the list of names and I'll call you back. Thank you."

He replaced the receiver and reached into his humidor for a cigar. He held it to his mouth and lit it and blew the smoke from his lips. He looked up and rose from his seat.

"I'm Glenn Becker, sir!" he said, standing before him. "You called for me."

"Yes! I sent for you because I hear that you have a sister by the name Sheena?" he asked.

"Yes, I do," answered Glenn.

"Well, for your sake, I would suggest that you keep her away from my son. This is my last warning if you want to keep on working here. I can promise you, I will make your life miserable."

Glenn's eyes opened wide. "What are you talking about?"

"Don't be smart with me, boy!" he threatened. "You damn well know what I'm talking about," shouted Steven angrily in his face.

Through the walls of the office, you could hear voices inside arguing. Glenn felt the anger rising to the surface. Part of him wanted to unleash it, but there was the other part of him that held back. His eyes were filled with suppressed anger and hate. He threw a big tantrum and said to himself under his breath, "My father was right about the Samson family. He has every reason to hate them all. First, his father, and now him. They are all the same. I must warn my sister not to have anything to do with them . . . Nothing!" Glenn stormed out of Steven's office, leaving the door opened.

"Come back in here! I haven't finished with you!" Steven roared. Glenn did not stop. He could not take any more of his rage or his threats. He quickly walked toward the lift. As he was about to enter the lift, he heard a voice called out to him. It was Jonathan. Glenn pretended that he did not hear him and entered the lift just before the doors were closing. Jonathan saw Glenn's eyes lit up with rage as he disappeared behind the sliding doors of the lift. Steven took out one of his fine cigars and cut the end off. He sat on the edge of his desk held his cigar between his thumb and forefinger and took a deep drag off it. The smoke he exhaled briefly wreathed his head in gray then drifted up to the ceiling. He turned, admiring his cigar. "A woman is only a woman, but a good cigar is smoke . . . Rudyard Kipling," he said while staring at it.

Jonathan suddenly paused, turned around, and headed to his father's office. The expression on his face was unexpectedly serious. He yelled furiously as he marched and swung the door open wide with papers in his hand. "What the heck is going on?"

Steven rose from his desk and stared at him and suddenly cracked like thunder. He said, "WHO THE HELL DO YOU THINK YOU'RE TALKING TO, BARGING IN MY OFFICE WITH THAT TONE?" He inhaled deeply before smashing his cigar in the ashtray on his desk. "YOU'RE NOBODY WITHOUT ME!" continued Steven.

"Nobody? I don't want any part of the company!" shouted Jonathan.

"Don't give me a reason to kick your ass out here! Now get out!" he snarled. "I don't have anything to say to you. Get out!" The volume of his voice rising with each word as his temper finally broke. "GET OUT!" he yelled.

The last repetition was pitched in such a furious tone that Shelia could hear them. Jonathan looked at him with utter disgust. "You just don't get it do you?" Some of the passersby heard them shouting from the office that they ran in, separating them, forcing Jonathan to leave the office. He threw the sheets that were in his hands on the floor and saying his last words while storming out the room.

"I don't want any part of this company. You can die and rot with it!"

Steven banged his first on his desk, responding, "There's a plane leaving every hour on the hour. Just get on one and get yourself a flight back to Seattle tomorrow!" shouted his father.

"Good! I'm getting out of here," he shouted back.

He hurried into his office, collected his jacket and car keys, slammed the door, and stormed out the office, heading toward the lift for the ground floor and out the building after Glenn. Jonathan decided to go to one of many bars nearby. Once outside, he crossed the road where he could see a row of stores, restaurants, and cafés. While walking, he bumped into a man carrying some papers, heading for the office building. The papers fell to the ground.

"Why don't you look where the hell you're going?" the man snapped.

"Oh, I'm sorry," Jonathan said as he continued walking.

"Hey!" yelled the man.

He stopped in front of a café. He walked in, and he found Glenn sipping a drink. From behind, he called out to him. Glenn was feeling bitter in spirit. He went up to him, touching his left shoulder before he sat down to talk.

"Glenn."

Glenn spun around toward the voice and looked at him as Jonathan pulled up a stool near the counter. He turned back to his drink, refusing to answer back. "Glenn, I'm sorry."

Glenn shook his head from side to side. "No! I'm not all right. Things are not looking so good for me after your father threatened me. Man, it's hard!" said Glenn. "The Samsons are hard people!"

"I understand you, but hey, I'm a Samson too, and I'm not the same as my father," responded Jonathan.

At that time, it did not make sense for Jonathan to stay on the island, so he decided to leave.

"Listen, Glenn. Tonight I'm leaving the island. I'm going back to Seattle."

He felt like he was in a large cage. Just then, his mobile rang. He took his mobile from a pocket inside his jacket, looking at the caller's ID before answering. It was Sheena. Glenn turned to Jonathan with a hard face.

"You're what?" Glenn said with a surprisingly shocked voice. "Seattle! and Sheena?" asked Glenn

"I know! I . . . I don't want to, but I just can't resist staying here any longer with my father. It's impossible."

"Come on now, Jonathan," Glenn said, raising his eyebrows. "You can't leave. You can't just walk away. You have to tell her."

His head snaps. "Really?" he shouted. "I don't have any choice."

"What choice? You don't have a choice."

"I know! *I know*! I wouldn't know how to tell her," sadly responded Jonathan "I'll be gone, and hopefully, she'll forget all about me."

"You must speak to her, Jonathan," advised Glenn. "You must see her tonight, and you must tell her."

"Okay, I don't want to hurt her. I love her!" responded Jonathan. "But it's for the best. I know I'm not worthy."

Even though he had agreed, in the end, he knew that doing so, their relationship would no longer be the same. The phone was ringing, and that brought Sheena out of the shower. Grabbing a large bath towel, she wrapped it around herself and ran through into her bedroom. Reaching for the phone, she said, "Hello, it's me. Hi, Jonathan!" she exclaimed, happy to hear his voice.

"We're still on for tomorrow, aren't we?"

"Why, are we supposed to meet?"

"Why, didn't your brother tell you?"

"Tell me what?"

"Okay . . . I need to see you. Is that possible?"

There was something in his voice that alarmed her, but knowing him the way she did, she knew he would be under pressure with work. She said, "No. What's wrong? You sound strange." He did not respond, then he cleared his throat.

"Not over the phone. I need to talk to you in person."

"Now?"

"No! Tomorrow, it's really urgent."

"What time do you want to meet?"

"Seven, if that's okay with you."

"All right," she agreed.

"See you then. I'll take you to lunch."

"Bye."

"Good night," he muttered and hung up.

Sheena stood with her hand resting on the phone, a puzzled look on her face. She sat heavily on the bed, shivering suddenly, even though it was a lovely evening and it was warm outside. Her heart sank. *Yes, that was it*, she thought. He was going to end their relationship.

Early the next morning, Sheena got up and went back to the bathroom, finished, and returned to the bedroom to dress. Since it was a lovely morning, she chose a light flowery orange dress.

Later that evening, Glenn went to Sheena's bedroom and told her that Jonathan wanted to see her. She smiled with joy and, at the same time, worry. She told him that he had already called, but she did not know the bad news. Glenn did not tell Sheena the reason why Jonathan wanted to see her. As soon as everyone was asleep, Sheena hurried downstairs and crept out of the house to meet Jonathan. A few minutes later, just before midnight, she left the house, knowing where Jonathan would be. Jonathan's jeep was already parked not too far from the house, near one of the fruit trees. As she arrived, heading to where Jonathan was, she braced herself, not knowing what he was going to say to her, not knowing what to expect. He was standing against the jeep. When he saw her, he smiled faintly. He made no move in her direction as he would normally do. She thought he looked drawn, and his eyes were dull without vitality.

"Hi," Sheena said.

He nodded. He cleared his throat and explained, "I don't know how to tell you."

Staring at him, she asked, sounding slightly perplexed, "What do you mean? What are you trying to say to me?"

"Today I had a discussion with my father."

"What were you talking about with your father?" asked Sheena.

"About us," responded Jonathan. "He knows everything about us."

There was a small pause before he continued, "Sheena, there's something else I must tell you, and I can't think of another way to tell you." Sheena looked at Jonathan's face and saw that it had completely changed. It was very serious; she was worried. She heard an edge on his voice all of a sudden and frowned.

"What's wrong?" She stared at him and waited patiently. He stood there; a deep sigh escaped him. Pain was in his eyes. He was going to tell her, but he had to find the right words.

"I really didn't want to tell you this. I just wanted us to be together, but I have to tell you something." He sighed again. "I'm leaving tonight for Seattle."

"Why now," asked Sheena. "For how long?"

"We've never had a proper talk, you and me. We were friends, and then we unexpectedly found ourselves tied to each other. We don't know very much about each other," he said softly, taking a step forward. The desperate look on her face made him desperate to comfort her. She pulled back with fear. "Sheena, I love you."

She did not respond and then said, "You're going to Seattle!" She was surprised, and you could see the hurt on her face. Tears filled her eyes and ran down her cheeks at the unexpected news; it was a heartbreaking time for her. She struggled free from his embrace. They stared at each other; she was not ready to let him go. She begged him not to leave.

"Don't be angry with me. Don't look at me like that. I've tried so hard to make my father understand, but I just can't. I can't Sheena. It's better this way. I can't see you anymore," confessed Jonathan. "I have to go. It's done. I don't want to see you. I don't want to be with you. I just want you to go."

"Please! How do you expect me to feel?" she exclaimed with tears running from her eyes.

"Please, Sheena, let me go!" Jonathan exclaimed.

He drew close to her, touched her face, then lightly kissed her, saying, "I'm sorry, Sheena, really sorry." Then he walked away, leaving her crying. Leaving her was one of the hardest decisions he had to make. She walked slowly toward her house, crying desperately. In the meantime, Glenn was in the kitchen, waiting. He saw his sister walking up to the door. He opened it, and he looked at her, the tears streaming down her face. Her mouth began to tremble.

"He doesn't love me anymore," she said. She was unable to continue. Glenn held his sister in his arms tight. Sheena felt rejected. Glenn closed the door behind her as she listened for his car to start and heard it drive away.

"He doesn't want me anymore." She sighed. "He never loved me."

They lightly walked up toward her bedroom, and he put her in bed. Glenn was angry, seeing his sister morally depressed, and was worried for her. That night, Glenn remained beside her until she cried herself to sleep. He left a side lamp on and covered her with a sheet and slept in an armchair.

Things were never the same after Jonathan had left her.

CHAPTER SEVEN

$\mathcal{T}$he following day, everyone was up except for Sheena. She skipped breakfast. For the family, it was normal that she remained in bed, but this time, it was different. Sheena had fallen into depression, standing in front of the window, staring out to nowhere, overcome by feelings of immense sadness and loneliness. Their story was over, dead, finished. Jonathan had given up. Back in the Samson mansion, Jonathan began to pack his cases with anger. That same night, when he was in bed, Jonathan couldn't sleep. He turned restlessly for hours. Back at the Beckers, Glenn tried to comfort Sheena, trying to help her understand that it was for the best that he was out of her life, but Sheena did not want to hear this from her brother. She sat up on the bed, staring at nothing as if her soul was drained out. She closed her eyes, remembering all the things he had said . . . that he loved her . . . that he was serious about her. It was not a game for him. Wet tears squeeze through her lashes and ran down her cheeks. Glenn left the room, so worried that he called his grandmother in secret. Datilda asked what was wrong with her granddaughter. Glenn explained.

Sheena got off the bed and walked over to a mirror hanging on the wall and looked at herself. Tear stains were on her cheeks. She did not want to see anyone, not even her grandmother. She was out of contact with everyone, drifting slowly away. Sheena was like a wounded animal licking her wounds.

As she lay on the bed, there was a knock on the door. She wiped her eyes. Datilda walked quickly toward her; she hugged her, saying, "Oh, my child! What has he done to you?" Sheena burst into tears. Datilda was worried if Leon was to suspect something. They had to make up a plan; the pain was unbearable for Sheena. Datilda stroked her hair, whispering, "It's all right. I'm here now. Everything's going to be all right." At lunchtime, Leon called everyone to join him at the table. Glenn and his grandmother were still in the room. they did not know what to do. Datilda sent Glenn to join the family and told him that she would join them later. From morning to evening, still, there was no sign of Sheena, and the family was starting to get worried. As Glenn entered the dining room, Leon turned to him.

"Where's your grandma?" he asked.

"She should be here any minute," Glenn answered.

"Where's Sheena?"

After about ten minutes, Datilda entered the room without Sheena.

"Where's Sheena?"

Datilda responded, "She feels better."

Leon was worried and asked his mother what was wrong with her. She knew but could not tell him. Coretta was worried too. She threw down the wooden spoon and rushed out of the kitchen to see what was wrong with her. Datilda followed her to the room. "My god, Sheena!" cried out Coretta. "What the matter with you? Why are you crying?" Coretta entered the room and found Sheena on the bed, crying desperately. She ran over to Sheena, Datilda went over to Coretta and told her that she was not well. Coretta walked over to the phone as she said, "I'll call the doctor." Datilda tried to calm her down, assuring that it was not something serious to be worried about, but Coretta was not convinced that she rushed out the room and called her husband.

"Leon! Leon!"

"What is it?" asked Leon.

"Call the doctor!"

"Why what's wrong?" cried out Leon, worried.

Everyone ran toward Sheena's room to see what was wrong with Sheena. Datilda told everyone that it was not anything to be worried about. Glenn stared at his sister and felt hatred grow toward Jonathan; he hated him so much that he wanted to beat him. In the meantime, Leon called a doctor to come to see their daughter. As the doctor visited Sheena, he noticed with sadness that she was showing signs of depression. Her delicate beauty seemed fragile. The sparkle of happiness had gone from her eyes; her ivory skin complexion was dull and pale. He sighed deeply. She felt herself drifting away. She focused on Datilda's mouth moving, but she could not make out what she was saying. As the doctor arrived, Datilda told everyone to leave the room, leaving her in the room with him. Datilda told the doctor to invent something up to avoid a serious problem in the family. He did not understand why, but he went along with it. The doctor closed the bedroom door gently behind him. As he was leaving, Leon went up to him and asked what the problem was. The doctor calmed the family by saying, "Don't worry, it's nothing serious. She'll be all right, now that I've given her something to calm her down. She's just going through a hormonal phase, and you all must let her rest as much as possible."

Datilda suggested that she would stay with her and make sure she ate. The doctor agreed that only Datilda should stay with her, and he left. Coretta was so sad she did not know what to do. Leon went up to her to comfort her.

"What's wrong with our child? Why is she acting like this?" asked Coretta, worried.

Datilda eased her worries, letting her know she must rest. She went back into the room and sat next to her on the bed. She put her arms around her and held her close. "Don't cry, Sheena. It's going to be all right." The tears came; slowly they trickled down her cheeks. "You must keep your strength up. Not eating is the worst thing you can do to yourself. You need nourishment. Let me bring something for you."

"I'm not hungry, Grandma."

A few minutes later, Datilda returned, carrying a tray with food on it.

"You must eat up, child!"

She wiped away her tears. "I'm not hungry, Grandma."

"You have to eat, child."

She picked up a fork full of rice and ate it.

"Bigger, Sheena," she insisted.

Sheena took another forkful.

"Bigger."

Sheena looked at her. "Grandma . . ."

"Don't worry, Sheena, everything will be all right." She watched her take another forkful.

"That's better."

Much later that night, when she was alone in her bedroom, she couldn't believe their relationship was over. *No,* she thought, *he cared too much.* Their story had been so intense, so passionate. She closed her eyes, remembering all the things he had said to her . . . that he loved her . . . that he was serious about her . . . that it was not a game for him. Why did he leave her if he had not meant what he said? She asked herself. He could have called from Seattle; he had access to phones wherever he was. *Well, of course, he meant those things when he said them,* the voice from the back of her head muttered. Suddenly, she felt like a fool. This may hit deep into her stomach; each word was a sharp knife. Tears sprang into her eyes; she wept for the loss of a man she loved, the life they would never share. It was a long night of tears.

She turned to look at her clock; it was 10:10 p.m. She sat up on the side of the bed for a moment, brushing them away, endeavoring to pull herself together, but it was impossible. Sheena had been sitting for days in her room, refusing to see anyone. Days and months passed, she waited for the phone to ring, hoping that he would call, but there had not been a slight word or call from him, not even a whisper from anyone, and that was a fact she could not ignore. She brushed the tears that sprung into her eyes aside as she turned to light a candle. As painful as it was, she had to admit that he left. He had swept her off her feet with his words, and he was never coming back. He was out of her life just like that—*puff*. She tried not to think about him, but it was useless. She had only to hear his name, and her heart started pounding, and her skin would tingle. She remembered her sister's wise words. She knew she was in love with him; she knew she wanted to be with him. But was that possible? She had loved him a lot, putting all of her trust in him. She had been so opened with him and honest, and at the end, he had deluded her. It had cut deep into her very soul. As painful as it was, she had to admit that it was over. Why? She would never know. Her gift of love meant nothing to him. She began to cry again, and she discovered that she could not stop.

Almost every day, Jalissa tried to phone her, but Sheena didn't move to answer. She wasn't in the mood to talk to anyone. Then Jalissa decided to go over to Sheena's fussing over her, but Sheena told her not to bother. She tried all she could to bring her back in the outside world instead of cutting herself from it.

"Is that what all everybody wants me to do, get on with my life?"

"We all just don't want to see you like this."

"I'm not going to give up on Jonathan."

"Of course not, and you shouldn't, but you must admit that your just letting your life pass by," she continued. "My mother once told me, actions make more of a statement than words ever could."

"Oh, Jalissa, do you think he will never think of me?"

"Hell yes!" she said, putting her arms around her, holding her close. "If he cared he would fight for you, if he doesn't, then he doesn't really love you." Jalissa answered. "And it would be better for both of you."

"It might be for him," Sheena said in a low voice, "but not for me."

Later, rumor got around to Eric that Sheena was not well and would not eat. Datilda tried so hard to force food down her. Eric showed up one day and asked if he could take Sheena out to the beach. Sheena responded she did not want to go, but her parents insisted that it would do her good than sitting at home. They did not know what to do with her, staying home, doing nothing. At the beach, Sheena's heart pounded and felt sick.

A couple of weeks later, Eric would visit her on a regular basis. She was struggling with her own pain. He asked Glenn what was the cause of her behaviour; Glenn could not confess Sheena's secret. Sheena could not see what was in front of her; all she had on her mind was Jonathan. As time went on, Sheena went to places every day, spending time with Eric, playing games in the family with her as they did when they were children. She started to recover from her depression and tried to forget him, realizing that there was only one thing to do, and that was to get on with her life. She then started to develop an interest toward Eric, at the same time, her secret was revealed to the rest of the family. After knowing why Sheena fell into depression, Eric felt anger toward Jonathan. One day, Eric went over to Glenn and told him how and what he would do if Jonathan ever went near Sheena again.

"I want to hear from his own mouth how he thinks it's noble to hurt someone, and then I want him to feel some real pain. I want him to understand what he put Sheena through."

Glenn had known Eric long enough to know he meant every word of what he had just said.

"Just leave it. Sheena has been through enough already."

"I have nothing to lose."

Eric came every day, and their relationship grew stronger, but Eric also developed a feeling for her that she did not know. He was, all the time, close to her, showing Sheena that he was always there for her. They were spending more time together, even though she found herself thinking of Jonathan constantly, talking, eating out, and strolling, but that did not change the way how she felt. She did not feel complete, and she was not ready to take it seriously. Days went by, most of them included a glimpse of Eric or a wave from him. After one great day at the beach, they sat and talked.

"I know there's something wrong. What's up?" He pleaded with her to tell him what was wrong; she bursts into tears and told him the whole story. He yelled at her and shook his head in disgust. "Why didn't you tell me? Don't you know that I've always been here for you? I would have gone after him and beat the hell out of him!"

That same evening, Eric decided to take her out for dinner. Sheena dressed casually since they were only going out. She was wearing a summery flowered dress. After the evening was over, they drove home in silence. There was nothing to talk about; they were completely comfortable in each other's company. Sheena got out the car, slammed the car door shut, and walked up the path. Eric walked her to the door, imagining what Sheena was thinking. He held her hand longer than it was necessary, and then he let it go before she felt too uncomfortable. He stopped, and Sheena turned to him. "Thank you," she said. "I had a great time."

He began to whisper in her ear, "Sheena, I'm your close friend, and I am willing to do anything for you. You were the one I wanted to go out with." Sheena was surprised; she did not know what to say. Eric leaned forward to kiss her; she took one step back and lowered her head. He was jealous; he knew that Sheena was still in love with Jonathan. Eric realized that she was not ready.

"I'm not ready, I need more time," she said. Jonathan was still on her mind.

"I don't feel just like a friend, Sheena . . . I feel more than a friend to you." Eric reminded her that Jonathan left her and that he was not coming back. As she entered her home, she replied, "I know."

"Look, Sheena, I'm sorry it didn't work out between you both, really, but these things happen, you know."

He stepped back and gave her a wave. Sheena watched him as he walked toward his car parked in front of her house before closing the door. He sat in the car, the key hanging from the ignition. He leaned his head against the headrest, thinking several minutes before starting the engine and driving off. He tried to be a gentleman; it had always been important to him to put a woman's need above his own. However, here, for some reason, he could not do it. He was not going to give up and drive off.

Everyone in the family could see that Sheena was herself again, smiling and talking, but at the same time, they wondered how she really felt. No one ever asked her. Eric continued coming to the house, hoping that she would not see or think about Jonathan again. Eric, this time, did not come to see Sheena on a friendly basis but to declare his feelings to her. Her father pretended that he did not know what was going on, being it was his idea. Eric approached Sheena and proposed to her. "I'm in love . . . with you. I just know I love you."

She was surprised. "I wasn't expecting I LOVE YOU. Don't look at me like that. I'm trying to find the right thing to say."

Eric felt embarrassed. He turned around to Leon; he did not know what to do. Leon was very angry with her. Datilda got up from her seat and protected her from her father and told Eric to leave. Leon walked over to Sheena and yelled at her, "What kind of manner is this? You should be polite after all that he has done for you." He understood her reaction toward Eric, but it was not acceptable. "Forget about that Samson. He left you, and not only that, he's engaged." Sheena could not bear the thought of him with someone else. Nine months had passed since she'd heard from him. For the first time in her life, she was in love with him. She shouldn't, but she was, and she did not know how to stop herself. She ran out into the yard and sat beneath a tree. Datilda went out and found her sitting against a mango tree; she walked over and sat next to her, stretching her legs out on the soft green grass. Sheena felt she could only speak to her grandma.

"Grandma, I'm so sad. I don't know what to do. I can't get him out of my mind . . . I still love him."

"Well, child, that's good," Datilda said.

"Yes, but Jonathan," she continued.

"He's good. I like that young man. I know that he thinks about you too," Datilda said with a smile. "He'll come around when the time's right. You just have to give him time, and I know you're hurting too, child."

CHAPTER EIGHT

After a couple of months back in Seattle, far from the island, Jonathan was leaning against his sweeping panoramic office window, thinking. He could remember, during his carefree life, there had been a list of things that he had done. There were women who had fallen into his arms as soon as he looked at them, women who flattered him or made him laugh, women who taught him things he had never dreamt of before.

There were his friends who wanted to drink with him all night until inevitably there was a headache or a hangover the next day and the feeling of regret after and those who took him racing. The following morning, Jonathan walked over to Alan's office for certain documents that he needed. Alan was a dark, Latin-looking with a shock of dark hair, black eyes, and a fresh complexion and was characterized as a womanizer with contagious habits. The two were close friends since school; they were not only friends, but also colleagues, and understood each other on a very fundamental level. And each worried about the other's well-being. They had a great deal in common. Nevertheless, despite their friendship, Jonathan had a love of truth and needed to find it. He knocked at the door and walked in, finding Alan leaning back in his office chair so far that Jonathan thought it was going to flip backward, clasping his hands behind his head, stretching his legs out in front of him on the desk while he was on the phone. Alan grinned at Jonathan, feeling comfortable and more at ease.

"What's up?" he asked.

Jonathan looked at him turned around and was about to walk out when Alan said, "Don't start that . . . I like a bit of female company." Jonathan walked toward the window, staring out; a warm feeling from deep inside his soul began to take form. In his whole life, Jonathan has never missed anyone the way he missed Sheena Becker. It had only been a couple of months, but to him, it seemed longer. Alan paused as he realized that he had lost Jonathan's attention. He barely heard what he was saying. All he could think about was that she was waiting for him.

"What's wrong?" he repeated.

"Nothing. Why?"

"You're not listening to me. You didn't hear one word I said."

Jonathan walked out and walked toward his office to write some notes. He walked over, sat behind his desk, turned on his portable computer, and connected to the network. He opened one of the four folders on his desk, which was containing information. Just as he was about to start, he leaned back in his chair. He thought for a moment about Sheena. He tried not to think, but he could not get her out of his mind. Pushing himself up off the chair, he walked toward the panoramic window and looked out. "I'll call her and explain," he said to himself, but he couldn't. Twice, he picked up the phone and thought, *What could I tell her? How could I explain?* He had no answer. "I'm going to do it!" he said to himself. He picked up the phone and dialed her number.

Back on the island, she had given up hope of Jonathan calling, when suddenly, it was a second or two, she heard the phone ringing. She had no idea who it could be. *Perhaps it was someone trying to get through*, she thought. She walked over to the phone and picked up the receiver.

"Hello." There was silence. "Hello!" she repeated.

Jonathan dropped the receiver back into its cradle and sat there for a while, staring at it, thinking. He did not want to seem anxious to call her. She placed the receiver down. Alan knocks on Jonathan's office door; a loud voice behind the door told whoever was there to go away. Alan knocked on the door again. He opened the door, poked his head around it, and half entered the room, raising his hand in greeting.

"I have been trying to get in touch with you. You have not been answering my calls. I wanted to apologize for this morning. I was rude."

"Are you all right? Can we talk?" he asked.

"You're already doing it."

"You want to tell me what's wrong. Did your father really tell you to leave?"

Without looking back at him, he nodded his head yes. Alan smiled. "I bet your mother's worried about you. "Don't you think she's worried about you?" he asks.

Destiny

"What do you think?"

"I have never seen you like this before, Jonathan."

"I've not been the same since I've been back. She's always in my thoughts."

"Wow! You mean a girl is the reason you're like this?"

"You're right about that."

"Jonathan, you and I are Mr. Ice. You have a heart of stone. I can't believe it. This is impossible."

"Nothing is impossible."

"By the way, your mother called, and I heard that you are in some sort of trouble!"

"Are you kidding me?" he blurted out. "What do you mean by trouble?"

"Your mother is very worried about you."

"I can't think why!"

"Well, to be frank, she told me you have become involved with a peasant on the island."

"Peasant?" Jonathan exclaimed. "How dare you call her peasant? Keep your mouth shut!" He could feel his blood race. He got up and stood behind his chair.

"You truly cannot be taking this really seriously! I don't know how long you've known each other, but, Jonathan, think about your mother."

"I'm not here to hear you talk about my mother, but business," said Jonathan as he looked at him.

"You act in a childlike way by breaking your mother's heart . . ."

85

Jonathan walked over to the window and looks at his reflection while Alan walked over to seat himself on the sofa.

"I've changed," he said. "For the first time in years, I've woken up."

"You could have chosen someone of your own environment," Alan said. "What makes you so sure she's the one for you?"

"I just know, trust me on this," Jonathan replied. "This one is different, Alan. You are a good friend, but leave me alone for once in my life. I have found someone who makes me feel good and alive."

"I am not here to criticize you. I am your friend," he said as he sits down. "Do you really love her?"

"I'll always love her."

"What does she look like?"

He looked at Alan and smiled. Alan stared at him, "She's the most beautiful woman, Jonathan said.

"So when do I meet the one who stole your heart?"

"Listen, it isn't easy," he answered. "In fact, it's very complicated."

"Look, I know how you feel, nonetheless, I think you should think about it."

He missed her, missed her warmth and affection, her sense of fun, her passion for life. She made him feel so alive in a way which he never felt before.

"Come on now, Jonathan. I'm really concerned about you."

"What's the point? It's not going to make me feel any better being here in Seattle." He began to shake his head. "No. I know

I'm not worthy. I miss her so much. I can't be what my father wants me to be. There's only so much I can take. This is me," he said, staring off into space for a moment. "Don't you understand? My father doesn't want me. He doesn't love me. He doesn't give a damn about me!" he yelled. "All he thinks about is his work."

"All right . . . What about her?"

"She's beautiful. No! She's very beautiful and warm and she's kind and she's caring. It's real. Honestly, when I'm around her, I forget who I am. Whatever strength I had before, it's drained.

"You're kidding me, right?" he blurted again.

"No, I'm not. I'm in love with her, but with my father, I am going through hell. We don't get on, and I've realized I have done something very, very stupid!" Alan nodded his head in approval.

Jonathan walked over to his desk, picked up a picture, and stared at it. A smile crossed his face and touched his eyes when he looked at it. Then he handed it over to Alan.

"Oh my god! When do I get to meet the future Mrs. Samson? She's beautiful," Alan asked. "You're so lucky, take my words for it. You're heading for the big one here, and you'll have a large battle on your hands."

Sheena was beautiful. Alan was amazed.

"Well then, whatever it is that is stupid, then I think what you need to do is adjust it."

"It's too late . . . I so badly want to find a hole to curl up into and fall asleep."

Alan rose to his feet. "It's not too late," he said quietly.

"How, then?"

"Phone her and tell her."

"It's not as simple as that. She is different."

"Well, Jonathan," Alan said in a firm tone, "the question is, are you going to sit here in your office and sulk about it, or are you going to do something about it? I wouldn't just sit around doing nothing . . . If she means so much to me . . . like you say . . . I would either call her, write her, or go to her, and just tell her really how much she truly . . . I mean, seriously means to me."

He came to a sudden decision. "Guess you're right."

"You have to leave this evening. I'll arrange your flight for you."

"Are you sure?"

"Yes, don't worry. I'll take care of everything here . . . just go."

"I appreciate that. I knew I could count on you. Thanks."

"Well, I want to be honest, Jonathan," Alan replied. "I have absolutely no desire and need to tie myself legally to a woman until I have to. I'm going to remain free and carefree until I'm old."

Jonathan responded, "You're my best friend, but don't you ever get bored?"

"Of what?"

"Yourself!" Jonathan said, smiling.

As Alan was leaving the room, he turned to Jonathan with a smile and said, "Good luck," and left. Jonathan walked to his desk and sat behind it. Through the walls of the office, he could hear the sound of traffic.

He began to write the letter. After finishing writing, he folded it and placed it into an envelope and was about to send it off when he decided not to; instead, he placed it in his bag. As he shuffled some papers from a file on his desk, he stopped and sat back in his chair, staring into space. He got up from his seat and walked over toward the panoramic office windows; leaning against it and gazed into nowhere, thinking of her. He could not get her out of his mind; she was everywhere. Fifteen minutes later, sitting down at his desk, he pulled the phone toward him and dialed Sheena's number; the phone rang. While Glenn was talking to his sister, Drusilla, in the hallway, they were interrupted by a ringing tone. She went over to the phone and answered immediately.

"Hello."

"Who's this?" Drusilla asked.

"Hello, it's Jonathan Samson."

Glenn, it's your friend."

Not knowing who it was, he walked over, picked up the phone, and spoke. Glenn's face changed with surprise that he wanted to put the phone down when he heard it was Jonathan. Drusilla stopped him, telling him to talk with him. Then he added in an icy tone.

"What do you want?"

"I want to talk to you."

"I have nothing to say to you."

Drusilla looked at her brother, telling him to listen to him.

"What do you want?" he asked angrily.

"I need you to do me a favour without questioning. I want you to help me. I know, Glenn! I made a mistake. I should not have left, but I must see her," responded Jonathan.

"She's not here," Glenn replied, ignoring his attempt of friendliness.

"When do you expect her to be back?"

"Listen, I don't know," Glenn replied, "so don't come back. Leave my sister alone."

"I can't," responded Jonathan. "I love her! During these nine months I reflected, I couldn't stop thinking about her."

"You should have thought about that before you left her!" he said with a feeling of betrayal. "She doesn't need you. She has forgotten you. When you truly love someone," Glenn said firmly, "you want that person to be happy. We heard that you're engaged too."

"Wait, who is engaged?" asked Jonathan surprisingly.

"Jonathan, please, man!" responded Glenn.

"I'm not engaged, and I have never been engaged," said Jonathan.

"Just leave my sister alone now that she's found herself someone else," responded Glenn and slammed the phone down.

The words that he heard coming from Glenn made Jonathan become jealous. It was the first time he had been consumed with jealousy. Sheena really meant something to him. He was afraid of losing her for good; he realized what he had done and decided to book a flight back to the island that night. Grace's phone rang; the maid answered it and called Grace. She excused herself from her guests, and she answered and found it was her son, Jonathan, on the line. After the conversation was over, Grace was worried. She walked to the lounge where she left her guests.

"Who was that?"

"Guess?"

"My son. He just called. He'll be flying back tomorrow morning."

They looked at each other, worried of Steven's reaction when he hears the news.

"Are you going to tell your husband?"

"No," responded Grace.

Early in the morning, Jonathan left for the airport in Seattle. He boarded his plane, sat down, and watched the plane take off. During the flight, Jonathan stared out of the window, wondering if Sheena would forgive him. The pilot announced their approach to the island; the plane floated downward and gently set down on the runway. On the landing and after stretching for a second, he looked out the window as they continued toward the big terminal. When the plane stopped finally, Jonathan thanked the crew members and the pilot as he headed out the hatch. He and the passengers made their way to the passport control, where the passports were checked by uniformed guards. Jonathan handed his passport. The guard flipped through it and handed it back to him. Jonathan then moved on through the airport administration. He grabbed his bags and settled them on a trolley and made his way through the crowd to the exit, and then he took a taxi home. While the night's coolness was still on the flowers, Grace went out to cut roses before her appointment, carrying two long, flat, English willow trug baskets and a sharp pair of secateurs from the greenhouse designed to hold flowers as they waited to be arranged. Soon, both baskets were piled high with roses. She turned and made her way back to the house.

Grace prepared herself and went into town for one of her visits. After the afternoon, she decided to have lunch with her friend, so the two women went to Pier One restaurant. Later, returning from lunch, the maid took her coat and bag and headed toward her room to leave them. On her way back to the lounge, where Grace was sitting, Grace told her to bring her a cool drink. Entering the house, Jonathan left his bags near the door in the hallway to greet and kiss his mother. As he was going to do so, the maid approached him.

"Welcome home, Jonathan. I trust you had a comfortable flight?"

"Very comfortable, thank you," Jonathan said.

Jonathan asked her where his mother was. As she was about to say, Grace showed up, walking to greet her son.

"You're back!" she said, smiling.

"Yes."

"Listen, go and rest, dear."

"I will rest later. I have to do something first."

He went up to his room to have a shower. Dazing into nowhere, he could hardly wait to see her and have his arms around her. He snapped out of it and turned off the shower. "No time for fantasizing," he said to himself. He reached for a towel and wrapped it around himself and went back to his room turned on the CD player and left the door open so that he could enjoy the music.

Returning to the bathroom, he stared at himself in the bathroom mirror. Jonathan ran a hand over his face; he needed a shave. He lathered himself with soap and scraped the razor over the sides of his face, rinsed, combed his damp hair, and then went back to his room, listening to music. Once he was dry, he got dressed quickly, choosing a T-shirt to go with his light linen trousers. "I love her!" he told himself. "Nobody, not even my father, is going to prevent me from marrying her!" Once he was ready, he went to turn off the CD player and left his room, running down the stairs.

"Jonathan!" cried out Grace while Jonathan rushed down the stairs.

"I'll explain later, Mother."

"But, Jonathan!" cried out Grace.

Before she could continue, Jonathan left her in the lounge, walked out through the door, and mounted his jeep. He sat at the steering wheel without moving for a few seconds. He placed the key in the ignition, pulled out of his yard, and headed in the direction of town. He thought, *What a beautiful evening.* It was cool and dry. Jonathan glanced out of the jeep's window and noticed the sunset in the background. It was the kind of evening that made him feel good to be alive, but he began to worry.

Opening the window of the jeep, he took a few deep breaths of pure air. Behind him, someone honked the horn; and rousing himself from his thoughts, he pressed his foot down on the pedal to accelerate until he reached town. Ten minutes later, he was driving into the car park. He breathed a sigh of relief and slowed down to park. He turned off the ignition and stepped out of his jeep. In the meantime, Coretta called Sheena. "Sheena, you are very, very beautiful," she said. "The Samson family would never consider you suitable for their son."

"And why not?" she questioned bluntly.

"Because where wealthy people are concerned, they marry their own kind, and that's the same with poor people."

"So to marry Jonathan, I have to be a daughter of a moneyed family!"

"Exactly," said Coretta. "And usually, the bride contributes something important to the marriage." She continued, "I'm sorry, Sheena, it's true. I and your father, we love you so much, and you should know you'll never be considered one of them. You have so much to learn."

"How can you be sure that what he is . . . is what he'll marry? I'm told by everyone, I am to have nothing to do with him," said Sheena with pain in her voice.

"He is a Samson," she said. "I do understand, child . . . I really do."

"How can you, if you've never spoken to him?"

"I don't need to, but remember this . . . action makes more of a statement than words ever do. Anyway, that's old and gone. There's Eric now."

Eric decided to take Sheena out to dinner to lighten the atmosphere. As they arrived in town, Sheena saw her brother sitting outside a club with some friends laughing and talking. They both went over to greet him and his friends. As they left walking to another club, ten minutes later, Jonathan on the other side was driving through the town. As he turned the jeep into another road, he looked into his rearview mirror, wondering what would be his next move. As he got out the jeep, he started to walk to the center, where there were a lot of people. Not far, he saw Sheena and walked over toward her. He appeared with a smile. Sheena cried out surprisingly, "Jonathan!"

"Hi!"

"What are you doing here?" Sheena replied sharply.

She looked at him with loathing.

"I'm here to see you, Sheena," he said. "I must speak with you."

Her heart thudded in her chest.

"When did you arrive back to the island?"

"This morning."

"And you came here to see me?"

"Yes, and I have no intention of leaving until I speak with you."

Eric was furious to see him. Sheena could not find her voice; her heart felt like it was going to swell up and burst through her chest. Jonathan gazed and turned to her, "I still think you're beautiful."

Eric went over to Jonathan, threatening him to stay away from Sheena.

"You left her, so back off!"

"There's no need to talk to me like that," Jonathan said. "I didn't come here to fight."

"If I were you," Eric said, "I'd just go on your way."

"I just need to talk to her."

"You have no idea who you're talking to!" The anger flared in him. "You don't come here on our island and pick who you want, and you can't just dump them when you want!"

"Listen, I don't know who you are, but I didn't come here to pick a fight with you."

In a fit of rage, Eric provoked Jonathan to fight, pushing him. Eric's right hand shot out and grabbed Jonathan's shirt.

"Back off," Jonathan blurted.

"Oh god!" screamed Sheena, terrified.

"Why?" He paused. "You want to take a punch?"

"Okay, come on, do it! Show me what you've got." He grabbed him by the arm. Jonathan tried to pull his arm away. Eric brought his nose to within inches of Jonathan's and, in anger, whispered, "Stay away from her or else!" he barked.

"Take your hands off me! I will not warn you again," warned Jonathan

Eric ignored him, laughing loudly, placing Sheena behind him. Clenching his fist in anger, he planted a right hook on Jonathan's chin. He fell toward the ground. The crowd surrounded them, shouting and cheering. During the first blow, Jonathan concentrated on his defense. After several minutes of attempts to get past Eric, Eric lost his temper and placed another jab. Jonathan did not see the blow coming. He went flying and hit something hard before falling to the ground. Jonathan staggered back and thought desperately a way to resist without getting hurt and told him not to touch him again. After a few minutes, the sweat poured from Eric's forehead. He planted another; Jonathan's hand formed into a tight fist and plants back another blow.

"Are you deaf?" Jonathan shouted. "I told you not to do that."

"You want to do something about it?"

"No," Jonathan responded, "I just want you to stop, that's all."

Eric smiled. "Then you're a yellow-bellied piece of shit. You think you Samsons own everything on this island."

"Whatever," Jonathan answered. "Just keep your hands off me. I'm not here to fight you in front of Sheena. If we must fight, we do it without her presence."

"Or what . . . what are you going to do?"

Not far from the scene, smaller crowds of tourists and passersby were drawn by the echoes of the two fighters. The public wondered which of the two would win. They were both wounded and bleeding; the two figures were fighting like wolves. Glenn went over to them. "Eric! Jonathan!" yelled Glenn as he stood.

Glenn jumped in between the two of them and tried to separate them. "That's enough!" yelled Glenn. "What the hell are you both doing?" he yelled again but was pushed aside by Eric. "Stop it!" Glenn shouted. "All you're doing is making things worse."

Jonathan tries to stop, but it was not easy. Eric's attacks took Jonathan by surprise; he struck him against chairs and tables outside a bar. Eric's anger was so strong that Sheena could feel as well as hear it. Jonathan gets up and struck back at him. Eric was stronger than him, but he was far from beaten. Eric's hand reached for Jonathan's throat. His thumb dug into his windpipe. His lips drew back to show his teeth. He came so close to his face that Jonathan could feel droplets of saliva spray on his face. He was ready to strike again. He plants another hook. After six blows, Jonathan, this time, ducked and caught his arm and snapped it. He moved one step backward while Eric fell to the ground silently, then things returned almost back to normal. People sat on the sidewalks, smoking, eating, and drinking as if nothing happened. Eric turned and looked at Jonathan in agony from the ground while Jonathan a few distances away on the floor. He stood up and walked over to where Sheena was standing.

"Sheena, stay with me," pleaded Eric. Jonathan glanced toward Sheena, who stood in silence, her hands clenched in painful distress.

Jonathan walked over. "Sheena, please don't cry," he said softly. She heard the embarrassment in his voice, but she heard the love and concern too. It had always upset him to see her cry. She lifted her head and looked at him. She stared at the cut above his eye. The blood ran down his face to his neck to the collar of his shirt. Meanwhile, Glenn told his friends handing over his car keys to collect his car and kneeled down to Eric to help him up. His car arrived; they both entered and drove off to the hospital.

"Sheena, I'm sorry. I hate to see you get hurt and unhappy. I love you . . . I love you so much . . . God, I've never loved anyone the way I love you."

Sheena knew she had undergone a vast change since meeting Jonathan. He brought out something within her that she no longer recognized herself; it made her very feminine and very much a woman. There was so much pain in her voice that Jonathan put his arms around her. He wanted to take away all the pain he had caused her, but how?

"I'm so sorry, Sheena," he said. "I was protecting you, and I just wanted to be sure about my own feelings."

He leaned to kiss her. She turns her lips away from his.

"You hurt me, Jonathan," she said. "When you left, I tried in every way to hate you."

"I know," responded Jonathan in a low voice. "I wish . . . I could undo what I did!"

"I'm not the Sheena you knew back then. I've changed."

"I expected that would happen," responded Jonathan.

Two hours later, Glenn returned, walking over to where they both were, trying to inform Jonathan what he did to his sister and all the problems she went through. Facing Sheena, he began to say, "While I was in Seattle, I spoke with your brother over the phone because I was coming back here, but he refused to see me. So I was left with no choice but to come and apologize in person. I'm really sorry for everything that had happened the day that I left. I told him that I was guilty for what I did to you. I know it isn't going to be easy for you to forgive me. I had no choice but to come back to ask for your forgiveness. Jonathan held her, gently gazing into her eyes. "I'm here. I knew that if I didn't come back, I would regret it for the rest of my life. I've missed you, Sheena. I swear I won't ever hurt you again. How can I convince you? I've learnt my lesson. I'm not lying. Don't you trust me?" Sheena smiled at him and exclaimed, "You hurt me, but I've missed you so much!

"I know, I really missed you," he said and brought her into his arms and kissed her deeply and passionately.

He took her and drove her to their secret place, telling her that he had to tell her something but couldn't do it anywhere else but the only place where their love started. The jeep stopped; they stepped out. She turned and went and rested on a nearby rock. He went over and sat down next to her; he turned toward her and declared, gazing into her eyes, "You're attractive, intelligent, there's something about you, Sheena . . . I've been waiting a long time to meet someone like you."

"I don't want us to be apart anymore . . . ever!"

"Me neither."

"Maybe this is what you call destiny," she said, smiling.

"Destiny?" Jonathan smiled.

She looked at him. "Yes, maybe it is."

He touched her face and whispered as he looked deep within her eyes, "I want you to know that I love you." They were so pure. He gave her a very gentle tap kiss on the border of her lips and pulled away. "I really do," he said. Then he put both his hands on the side of her cheeks and ran his finger up through and past her ears and through her hair. "I have another good reason for coming back here," he said. He took her hand. "Sheena, will you marry me?"

She pulled away; her heart began to beat faster. She was speechless. "W . . ." Her mouth opened with surprise. "What are you saying?"

"Must I say it again?" Jonathan replied, smiling. "I love you. I know I have been a complete idiot. I loved you from the moment I saw you, and when you told me you loved me, I felt—I told you before—alive like I've never been before, and I wish this more than anything I've ever wanted. I'm serious. Will you marry me, Sheena?"

She looked up at Jonathan and felt her eyes fill with tears.

"I love you too."

"Why do I have the impression that there is a *but*?" he said slowly. "I thought that you and I might have something going. This was the beginning of something special. I love you more than anything else, and you love me too. I want to have another chance. What's wrong?"

Sheena said nothing.

"I guess I was wrong to think you were the one for me," he said, pulling back.

"I was thinking perhaps my parents are right, rich marrying the rich," she said. "We come from two different worlds, you and I. We can't continue. We just can't."

"I am not marrying your family," Jonathan said, "but *you*! And you are not marrying my family but *me*!"

"Be honest," she said. "How do you really feel about me, Jonathan?"

He put his finger under her chin and turned her face up to his. "Listen," he said, "from the moment we saw each other, we both knew something had happened to us, and it is something that has never happened to me or you before. You're the best thing that has happened to me in a long time."

"We can't go on forever, believing that no one is aware of what we are doing. She warned. "The village has eyes and ears everywhere, and sooner or later, rumours will spread, and my father will give me a lecture about not seeing you again!"

"Why should anyone know?"

"Even the birds and bees gossip . . . I am frightened!" Sheena responded.

"Are you trying to tell me that you do not wish to see me again?" Jonathan asked. "I have no wish to hurt you, I swear," he repeated. "I went away not because I didn't want you, it was because I didn't know how to have you."

Sheena said, interrupting him, "No!"

"Then why not?" he asked. "This is the most important thing that has ever happened to both of us."

"So much has happened and I . . . I got to know," Sheena demanded.

"Know what?" he asked.

"Rumours say you are engaged to be married. Is it right?"

"That is not true!" he responded with surprise. "Who told you this?" he asked. "My father has been trying to get me engaged ever since my grandfather died, for the sake of the company."

"And you agreed?"

"No. For god's sake, Sheena, there is not a woman in my life. You know. I just attend meetings and go to dinner parties, that is all. Yes, there've been a few women from the past but never had a serious relationship. I'm in love with *you*! It's impossible for me to think of marrying someone else," he said. "If you think anyone can stop me from marrying you, you are very much mistaken. Only you can do that."

She looked into his eyes and said, "Promise me you will not leave me. I love you."

He smiled and gave her a very gentle tap kiss and said, "I promise that I will never leave you again. I am always going to be here for you." He went on, "The only thing that really matters is that I want you to be my wife, and nobody shall stop me from having you. While I was in Seattle, I couldn't stop thinking about you. I wanted to send you this letter, but I decided to give it to you personally."

Barely breathing, she took the letter, opened it, and began to read the words and couldn't tear her eyes away. She felt like weeping with happiness.

Seattle

March 25th,

Sheena, when I am alone here in Seattle, I find myself thinking about every moment we spent together. The thought that has filled my mind is that you are not with me now, but I can almost feel you beside me as I write this letter. I've loved you from the first moment that I laid my eyes on you. I realize that you are the one I have been looking for. I want you and always will, and there is nothing that will ever change the way I feel about you.

The next few lines blurred as her eyes filled with tears, but after a few minutes, she went on reading.

Sheena, for the first time in my life, I have something to believe in. You give me the reason to fight for it. You mean everything to me despite our opposite backgrounds. You are my life now. You are the most beautiful thing that has happened to me. You've touched my life like an angel . . . My world without you is nothing. It would be completely empty. I feel your sadness and the ache in my heart. I've come to understand that a broken heart is the strongest heart. I don't think I've ever seriously told you how much I really loved you, Sheena—with all my heart and soul and mind. I don't want to lose you to anyone else now that I've found you. My greatest pride and joy are that you become my wife as I your husband forever. You would make me the happiest man in the world.

Jonathan

She stood there for a long time, holding the letter; and then she folded it carefully, placing it back in the envelope. She looked at him from under her eyelashes. He took her in his arm and gazed into her eyes and kissed her lips and pulled away. "Will you—"

She cut him off, "Jonathan; I . . . I love . . ."

He pulled out from his jacket pocket a little blue box. Opening it with confident hands, he revealed a glittering ring. She hugged him tightly. "I'll take that as a yes," he said, smiling.

"Yes," she whispered. She leaned forward and kissed him. "Of course, I'll marry you."

He went down on his knees and placed the ring on her finger. He looked at her eyes; her eyes were soft and shining with happiness. He put both his hands on the sides of her cheeks and ran his finger up through and past her ears and through her hair, then he brushed her cheeks with his thumb. Her eyes were closed; he stared at her eyelids until they came open, then he smiled as he pulled her slowly toward him. He pressed his lips to her mouth and kissed her gently but passionately moving from side to side until they were both breathless. Everything around her body became in existent. Her legs didn't move; they felt as if they no longer existed. He was kissing her as if he would never let her go. When he did release her lips, he hugged her. Jonathan held Sheena's hands then, in front of her, said, "I love you, Sheena, and I'm so sorry." He bleated, gazing into her eyes. "I'll never do that again, I swear."

She knew it would take some time before she could forget what had happened. Gently, he placed her face on his hands, leaned forward until his lips touched hers. "Only you, Sheena." Slowly he let his hands drop. He drove her home and asked that evening, "Do you object if I go and talk with your father about us?"

She stood in silence for a moment; she had a thought running through her head before responding, "No."

He kissed her good night at the gate.

CHAPTER NINE

That evening, in the Samsons' dining room, it was getting late for dinner, and there was no sign of Jonathan. Steven and Grace were talking, when Steven reached across the table and gave Grace's hand a tender squeeze.

"Are you sure he is going to be here?"

"Yes, darling," replied Grace.

Grace and Steven decided to start without him. Finally, Jonathan appeared.

"It's about time, Jonathan! What happened?" she asked.

"Is this how you respect your mother?"

Steven noticed something; he got up from his seat and rushed over to his son, placing his glass on the table, and took hold of him by the arm. "What's this above your eye?" Grace's expression was twisting with the mother's sympathy, pains, and concern as she took in the damage of her son. Jonathan tried to hide his face.

"I got into a fight, that's all," he said.

"A fight!" Grace reached out to touch the cuts above his eye. He moved away from her.

"You look like as if you took on a bull!"

"It's nothing," he said, moving away from them. "Don't make a big deal out of it, Mother." "Nothing? How can you say it's nothing?"

"'Cause . . ."

Fifteen minutes later, the doorbell rang. Grace sighed and turned; as Charlotte approached the room, her entrance had brought everyone's attention.

"Yes, Charlotte?"

"Madam, the police are here."

Steven charged over to the door. "What are you doing here?" he demanded. The officer smiled.

"It's kind of late, sir. I'm here to see your son."

Grace turned toward Jonathan, her heart thudding in her chest. Grace met the police's gaze and felt a terrible sensation in her stomach.

"Jonathan Samson," the police officer said, "we received a police call that there was a fight in town. We are here to press charges against this person."

"I have no wish to press any charges against this person," Jonathan said.

"But, son!" said Grace.

"I can't believe you're saying this," Steven said. "There were witnesses . . ."

Jonathan cut him off with a look.

"Okay, sir, but if you change your mind, you know where to find us," said the officer.

"Good night," he said and walked away.

They went back to the dining room and sat around the table. Grace then said, "I had no idea that you were here from Seattle!"

"I arrived this morning."

Steven looked at Grace. There was no chance of saying anything. Jonathan decided to go to bed early and kissed his mother good night on her cheek. Steven only glanced at his son as he walked past him toward the stairs. Grace and Steven were alone in the lounge. He straightened, reached for his glass of wine, and grimly sipped until Grace said she would go to bed.

"I shall go to bed also," Grace said. "There is so much still to do tomorrow . . . Don't stay up too late darling."

She realized that her husband was not listening, so she walked toward the stairs and climbed up slowly toward her room. There was nothing more he could do that night. He placed his glass on the side table and walked toward the stairs to his room. As she began to undress, she found herself thinking. She thought that her son and Sheena were well suited to each other. She knew her husband would never accept their relationship. The next morning, everyone was up, and news got round that the Samsons' son was back, and there was a fight between his son and Eric Sànchez. Leon couldn't stand the idea of his daughter with the Samsons' son. He wasn't happy with Sheena. Every time she attempted to mention Jonathan's name, Leon made a certain face of this approval even with anger.

"He's good, gentle, and sensitive. He cares about me. I love him, and he loves me. I'm twenty-five, and I know what I'm doing. I'm very lucky to marry him," said Sheena.

Leon looked at his wife; they were shocked! After a moment of shock, Leon responded:

"What . . . lucky?" Leon laughed. "You're crazy!"

"Yes, Paps, he has asked me to marry him, and I'm also wearing his ring."

Leon didn't approve of her choice in marriage, nor did he understand her love.

"I'm serious," Leon replied. "You have no idea of his family!" Leon yelled.

"But, Paps, he . . . you don't even know him. We've known each other more than eight months," responded Sheena.

"Eight months behind our backs!" responded Coretta with shock. "You told us you didn't even know him. You have no respect for us, Sheena, after all we've done for you!"

"Yes, I have, and I'm sorry," she said. "He cares for me, and nothing else matters except the love from my family," replied Sheena.

"Sheena, you have not even met many young men," Coretta said gently. "Marrying is a very big responsibility."

Sheena closed her eyes and counted to ten before replying.

"That is exactly what I expected you would say," Sheena replied. "I am not doing this to upset you both. I need to do this for myself. Can you both understand that? Am I not old enough to be in love?"

"Did you accept?" Coretta inquired.

"If it was Eric, you wouldn't respond in such a way. You would be happy for us."

"That's different," responded Leon.

"What's different?" she asked. "It's because he's the son of the Samsons."

"Yes," said her mother, "when love comes, it is something overwhelming, so different from anything else."

"But he . . ."

"I don't care!" she replied, waving her hand in the air.

The same evening, back at the Samsons mansion, as Jonathan entered the house, Grace called him, "Jonathan!"

"Good evening, Mother."

"I need to talk to you, dear."

"What's wrong?" asked Jonathan.

"Is it true you were involved in a fight yesterday evening over that girl?" Grace asked, worried. "You know I dislike listening to gossip, but I received a call saying so. It's impossible to ignore them too."

Jonathan broke the news to his mother.

"Mother, I love you, and I value your opinion. I realize Sheena is not from our culture, but I care for her. I'm going to marry her, and I want your blessing"

Grace disagreed of his choice, thinking that she was not good enough for her son.

"Jonathan, you're asking me to go against your father's will, and you know I can't. And at the same time, I don't want to lose my son."

"Mother, you're not losing a son, but you're gaining a daughter," he said with a smile on his face.

CHAPTER TEN

$\mathcal{S}$ unday morning, half an hour later after the Sunday service, Sheena was on the phone with Jalissa, asking to see her tomorrow morning. Jalissa was offended by the fact that Sheena kept her secret.

"Hi, honey!"

"Hi, Jalissa! What's up?"

"I needed to talk to someone."

"Okay. What time?"

"Nine, all right?"

"See you tomorrow morning."

"Okay."

The following day, Sheena gets ready and goes out to meet her friends.

"Hi, guys!"

"Hi, honey. What's wrong?"

"What did you do with your hair?" said Shakeia.

"Do you like it?" Jalissa asked with a smile. "New look, new style!"

"Yeah, it's cool," said every one.

"Where's your tan, Jalissa?" Cattleya asked.

Cattleya held Jalissa's arm up for inspection. Her skin was almost as fair as Shakeia's.

"I thought you would be tanned, Jalissa!" said Cattleya surprisingly.

"You know I never tan," responded Jalissa. "What's up, Sheena?"

"I'm sure you've heard the rumours about me," she asked.

"Yes, and I'm surprised that you didn't say anything at all to us about it."

"I know, but I couldn't know everyone was against the idea, but it's not what I planned or I had in mind. It just happened," she said.

"But still, Sheena, you could have told us. We're your friends," explained Jalissa.

"He's different," she said.

"Yeah, yeah, it's just money," said Cattleya.

"What are you talking about?" she said puzzled.

"Snap out of it, Sheena. We're talking about your relationship with him. You're from two different worlds. It wouldn't work," said Shakeia.

"Please don't say you're in love," said Cattleya.

"Tell us it's not true," asked Cattleya and Shakeia.

"How dare you!"

Jalissa jumped in the discussion, telling the other two friends off and not being happy about the fact Sheena kept her secret from them.

"Guys, so go to hell with all that rubbish about two different worlds, anything is possible," said Jalissa.

"All the same, she can't marry him. Your father would never permit it," Cattleya said, walking off, smiling in a sarcastic way.

Jalissa turned to Sheena. "Hey, honey, look at me, you should have told me. It was something really serious," she said in a warm voice. "I would have been there for you."

"Forgive me, yeah?" Sheena said.

"Yeah, I forgive you," Jalissa said with a smile and a hug. "Anyway, what's wrong?" Then she walked to one side to talk with her, leaving the others.

"My parents, but especially my father, he just won't listen to me. He's completely against our relationship. I've tried so many times to get them to spend time with him and get to know him so they can see and understand that he's not like his father, but instead, my father has refused to have anything to do with him. Jonathan has also tried to speak to him. Things are really wonderful between us, and I feel confident that he is the right person I want to spend my entire life with, but I don't know what to do, Jalissa!"

"I've never seen you so unhappy."

"I really don't know what to do. Help me."

"I really don't know what advice to give you, have you . . ."

"Do you think he'll want to marry you?"

"I don't know . . ."

"Do you still love him?"

"I'll always love him."

Jalissa went up to her and put her arms around her; she could not stop sobbing. Sheena clutched Jalissa as if never to let her go.

"What I can only say, Sheena, is if you know he is the right person for you, then the stronger and honest you both are with them, the better."

"You seem so sure."

"At the end of the day, Sheena, love endures all things and never fails," she said. "When it's real, you can't walk away."

"I'm afraid."

"Honey, why don't you just wait and see what happens . . . Maybe he will come to his senses."

Jalissa smoothed her hand down Sheena's arms to comfort her. After a while, the sobs lessened, and Sheena grew calmer. Jalissa took a tissue from the pocket that was in her bag and wiped Sheena's eyes, then they both drew her into a circle of their arms, hugged, and kissed her on her cheeks.

"Go for it girl. This is who you really are, let's go out tonight."

"I could do with a girls' night."

"See you at ten then."

"Okay."

Jalissa pulled away and looked toward Cattleya's face. They both went their separate ways. Sheena walked back to the house, thinking about the situation they would be facing.

About two hours later, Jalissa went to pay Cattleya a visit.

"What's wrong with you, Cattleya?" Jalissa asked. "Why are you so hard with her . . . I keep telling you she's our sister, and she needs us."

"What do you mean?" she asked as if she didn't know.

"Don't play dumb!" she said. "Don't let us quarrel. You have something against Sheena. Spill it!" Jalissa said.

"Nothing!" Cattleya said, struggling to keep her voice steady.

"It's not just nothing, we are supposed to be all friends," she said. "I don't like it. I can't help if I don't know what's wrong," Jalissa said worried.

"I said there's nothing!"

"Don't tell me you're jealous of Sheena . . . It's that, isn't it?" she said. "The problem lies in the fact that Sheena found someone," she continued.

"Jealous! Jealous of what?" said Cattleya sarcastically.

"You tell me!" said Jalissa and walked off.

Evening came, and Cattleya decided to see Sheena before the others arrived. As Sheena was coming down the stairs, there was a knock at the door. She opened it and surprisingly found Cattleya standing in the doorway.

"Hey!"

"Hi. Are you okay?"

"No, a lot of things have happened. Jonathan's father has been doing everything to tear us apart."

"I couldn't wait any longer to talk to you," she said. "I feel guilty. You're obviously upset about your situation and my attitude toward you. I just walk away, that's not me. I'm sorry, you're my best friend, Sheena!"

"You're just being a friend."

"No, I'm not . . . I'm not being a good friend at all, Sheena."

"Maybe it's for the best. If you need me, I'm here for you, and I'm sorry. I couldn't show you that yesterday. I know that you and Jonathan are going through a tough time," Cattleya continued.

"I broke up with Jonathan."

"I have something to tell you."

"What is it?"

Cattleya hesitated, cleared her throat, and said quickly, "You'd better know this even though it might hurt more than ever. There were other rumours . . . Jonathan is engaged. I found out just two days ago, but I didn't want to tell you then and upset you. However, I thought you should know." There was silence between them. Sheena looked at Cattleya, wondering if she told her for spite or as a friend.

"Who told you this?"

"A friend who works for the Samson Company."

"Are you sure?" Sheena asked.

"Yes. Are you okay?" Cattleya said, walking over to hug her as Sheena weeps. This hug was warm on both sides.

CHAPTER ELEVEN

*A*s the evening progressed, the family sat at the dinner table. The atmosphere was different. Her father was not pleased about the relationship with her and the Samsons' son. Her mother worried about her husband, her grandma trying her best to distract everybody away from the problems. After eating, they all rose from where they were sitting and walked toward the door, facing the garden. Sheena went to her mother and told her that she was going out with her friends and climbed up the stairs to her room to prepare herself. She took out the blue dress that Jonathan had given her as a present and placed it on her bed. She went in the bathroom to wash and prepare herself. In the meantime, her mother walked into her room and stopped abruptly as she saw the silky satin dress lying on the bed. She picked it up, touching it with her fingers. When Sheena walked in, she was afraid what she had to say.

"Where did that come from?" Coretta asked in amazement.

"Jonathan gave it to me as a gift."

"Give it back to him," she said. "You can't have this in the family. He's insulting us."

"No, he's not! He loves me," Sheena said.

"Girl! You don't know these people. We can't afford something like this, and you can't accept something like this from him either," she said.

"I want to wear it tonight with my friends."

"Your friends can't afford something like this, and you want to go out with them with this?" he shouted as he stares at her. "Sheena, you should know better by now."

Sheena felt guilty that her mother might be right. Her father stood in the doorway and saw Coretta holding the dress in her hands. He stared at it, took it, tore it, and threw the dress on the floor before walking out the room. He told her to put one of her dresses that they bought for her. There was so much pain in her voice that her mother put her arms around her.

"I'm sorry if I have made it worse," she said. "But I was defending you against any unhappiness."

"I love Jonathan," Sheena said. "I have loved him since the first time I met him here in our home."

She felt sad that the only present she had from him couldn't be worn. It was nine; her friends were in the house, waiting and talking to the rest of the family. Sheena's eyes were downcast while walking out the room. Jalissa noticed the expression on Sheena's face but pretended that she did not notice it. They all greeted Sheena's family before leaving. Driving into town, there was the usual crowd of young prostitutes working the streets just outside the cafe. Jonathan was in town too, driving, looking at all the passersby, prostitutes trying to woo the single male tourists. In the opposite direction, Sheena and her friends were driving in town. They parked the car and started walking. Jonathan noticed Sheena and flashed his lights. Jalissa asked Sheena if she knew who it was; she turned and told Jalissa it was Jonathan.

"Oh my god," Shakeia whispered.

"You can say that again," breathed Cattleya.

"Who is that?" said Shakeia.

"That's Jonathan," Sheena said.

"He's perfect!"

"Oh, come on, Shakeia. You've already got someone after you. What more do you want?"

Jalissa was shocked by the fact that Jonathan was stunning. She smiled and told her it was okay to go to him. Jonathan had locked his jeep and started to walk up to Sheena. She walked up toward him, leaving the other girls right behind. As she was getting closer, he noticed that she was sad.

"What happened?"

"I couldn't wear your dress," said Sheena sadly.

"Why?"

"Because my father took the dress, tore it, and threw it on the floor." A tear ran down her cheek. She paused silently for a while and said, "My mother said I couldn't have that dress. We can't afford something like that."

He held her as she broke into a silent sob. He did not quite know what to say. He told her that the dress was not a big deal, and she had no reason to be upset. He wanted to tell her that he would buy her another dress or that she could depend on him for anything, but he held back as it was not going to sound right. Instead, he said, "I'm sorry. I didn't think when I bought it what problems it would have caused you." She quickly straightened up her back and pulled herself together.

"Sheena, I must talk with your father about us. I will come to your home tomorrow morning."

"I've tried talking to him myself, but it's no use."

"I will not give up!"

They walked through the streets and, for several hours, held hands, hardly speaking, then they decided to leave the town and go to the beach. It was a beautiful evening, they took a walk along the shore with their bare feet, holding hands under the stars that night. There were a few people walking along the shore. In the background, there were the soothing sounds of waves lapping as they rolled up on the shore. At one moment, Jonathan stopped and turned to face her, looked down into her deep, mysterious eyes. "Sheena, I'm so happy!" he exclaimed. "Happier than I've ever been for years." He grinned at her, pulling her to him. "I love you," he said, his mouth on her ears. "I love you, Sheena Becker."

Walking away, Sheena said, "And I love you, Jonathan Samson."

"What did you say? I didn't hear you!" he shouted back with the roar of the ocean in the back ground.

"I LOVE YOU JONATHAN!" she screamed at the top of her lungs as she was running.

At the end of the beach was a large rock. He ran after her, caught her around her waist, placed his arms around her, and directed her toward it, and sat down. Jonathan felt a sudden rush of happiness surging up in him. It never ceased to amaze him that she could arouse such passion in him. He knew it was because of Sheena. "I'm glad we met. I'm happy you're here with me." He stopped and caress her cheek, looked at her with a faint smile briefly touching his mouth. "You're the best thing that's happened to me in a long time." He kissed her on the tip of her nose. The evening sea breeze was cool. He kept his arm around her and rested her head against his shoulder. It was beautiful, so breathtaking, they thought as they sat staring at the sunset.

After a moment, she reached out and took hold of his hand tightly in hers. They got up and walked back the way they had come, retracing their steps.

CHAPTER TWELVE

*N*ext morning, Jonathan left his house not having breakfast and headed to the Beckers' home. Datilda could no longer bear the atmosphere of war between the two families, so she decided, without telling her son, that she was going to the Samsons, a place about some few miles drive out from the city on the other side of the island. She decided to leave the house by taxi late afternoon to town. She leaned forward and said to the driver, "I need to make a stop at the Samson mansion, please."

"Okay," responded the driver and headed east.

When the driver arrived, he parked the taxi in front of two open huge, tall, painted iron steel gates formed as lions. She stepped out of the taxi and told him to wait for her, walking toward the gates. She walked up to the gate and rang the bell.

"Yes, may I help you?" came the woman's voice from the speaker.

"I am sorry to bother you. I have been driving on the road about an hour from here. I was hoping to talk to the mistress of the house," Datilda said into the intercom.

"Hang on," came the response. The gate opened, and Datilda made her way in. A door opened in the small guardhouse next to the fence, and a man came out.

"Come in here for a moment while I call the main house and make sure it is okay for you to go on up there. May I have your name please?"

"My name's Datilda Becker."

The man was huge, obviously a bodyguard. He had more muscles than some of the bodybuilders. He definitely would scare away any with just a look, but his voice, when he spoke, told a different story. He had a kind voice, and the way he was looking at her was like he was genuinely worried. She was old and tired. She heard a voice on the phone. "Madam, this is Jack Brandon at the front gate. There is a visitor named Datilda Becker. I was wondering if there is anyone who could come down here to take her up to see you." Datilda listened to the one-sided conversation.

"Yes, Charlotte."

"Please send her up."

"Okay, I will send her right up. Thanks." Jason hung up the phone.

Jason helped her up and opened the door for her.

"Thank you again," she said as she began walking toward the house slowly. Datilda, being old, wasn't able to walk quickly. The Samsons' property was huge, a beautifully styled house with a large front porch and columns along the front, sitting on eleven acres of land. In front, there were two rows of tall and stately elms and a long avenue leading to the house where she started to walk up the path. Grace had left the front door open when she had come in from the garden after she had been picking flowers and was arranging them in vases. The gardener sent by Charlotte went to meet Datilda while walking toward the house. The gardener arrived and began to ask, "Who do you want to speak to?"

"The mistress of the house," replied Datilda

He led Datilda by his arm up to the entrance of the house, where Grace was standing. Grace stood in the doorway, looking at her. She was shocked to see a face. She knew this was not the first time that Datilda had ever been to the Samsons' mansion.

"You must be Grace Richardson, the daughter of Joseph Murphy Richardson."

"Yes, if you know who I am, I can only ask you kindly to introduce yourself."

"My name's Datilda Shawn. Becker was my husband's surname."

"I must ask you to leave."

"I won't leave until I've talked to you."

"You must leave my premises now!" yelled Grace.

"No, I said, I need to talk to you."

Grace felt guilty. Datilda was old, and she looked tired. "Come inside," said Grace, walking quickly. "I was just arranging the flowers in the vases. I cannot bear a room without flowers."

"Thank you."

In the meantime, Jonathan arrived at the Beckers' home, hoping to find Sheena's father in. He went up to the front door and rang the doorbell; there was no answer. He rang again; he could hear someone coming to unlock the door. As the door opened, there standing in front of him was Sheena's father. Jonathan was not afraid of him; he had come with intention to see him. He could see in his eyes he was not an easy man to talk to, but he was willing to face him on an important matter. Asking Sheena to marry him wasn't a problem. What was worrying him was asking her father. *Will he give his blessing?* When Leon saw who it was, he was about to close the door on him when Jonathan placed his foot in the doorway.

"You must forgive me, Mr. Becker," he said, "for calling so early in the morning, but I have to talk to you if you just could hear me out."

"No! I don't want to listen to you."

"I love Sheena, and I'm asking you, but not in this way with the door in my face," Jonathan said.

"Marry! You people don't know the meaning of love or marriage, just money. You even insulted us by giving something to Sheena that we can't afford for our own daughter," responded Leon.

"I am sorry. I didn't mean to disrespect you. I didn't think at the time, but truly I love her."

"No, it's not that you did not think. You don't care."

"With great respect, Mr. Becker, I love Sheena, I really do, despite the conflict our families have. I love her. Don't think my father is pleased about the fact I am in love with your daughter. No matter how long it takes, I will fight for her," said Jonathan.

"Well, you said what you came here to say. Now you can go."

"I will keep coming until you listen to me," responded Jonathan.

Jonathan took his foot away from the doorstep and didn't continue. Leon closed the door and turned to go up the stairs to his room when he found Sheena standing at the top of the stairs. Her eyes grew with anger and walked away toward her room, closing the door behind her. Back to the Samsons' mansion, Datilda followed Grace to the lounge. She began to notice with particular interest a portrait of Grace's father, Joseph Murphy Richardson, and her mother, Cecilia Collins, which hung in the lounge above the fireplace. Her father, she knew when she was young, he was a gentleman, medium height, narrow shoulders with strong features, keen, blue eyes, intelligent and with speck of courage. There were, in the house, many other valuable antiques. As they were walking, Grace began to ask more questions about her visit.

"Tell me the reason of your visit."

"We have something in common."

"What's that?" asked Grace. "I can't see that we do."

"Whatever it is that you're thinking, it's not that, but your son, Jonathan, and my granddaughter, Sheena," replied Datilda.

Grace stopped walking, seated herself in a chair by the fireplace opposite Datilda, and said with a tone of distance, "I understand that my son, despite the fact that he is engaged to be married, has become somewhat involved with your granddaughter!"

"I'm too old to fight, I'm not well. I love my granddaughter so much as you do your son, and this is something that you and my family cannot destroy—Love! It's a blessing from God."

"You love your son, don't you?"

"Yes, I do."

"If you really love your son, then why do you want to destroy what God has given? Don't destroy it. It's no use fighting against it; you will only lose your son."

"My son, I'm pointing out that my son comes from an aristocrat family!"

"I have never heard such foolish nonsense!" she replied. "Where there is love, that's what matters more. I remember Steven's father and your father, and I'm sure they wouldn't be so firm with their only grandson." Datilda looked at Grace's face; the expressions in her eyes were hard. She responded, "What I'm asking, Grace, is that you help try to persuade your husband to accept their love, or you'll regret it later by losing him," she continued.

"How dare you enter my house, ordering me to go against my husband!"

"I didn't come here to argue with you, child," she said in a soft tone. "My intentions were only to appeal to you about this situation."

Grace interrupted the conversation.

"I think we have nothing further to say to each other on this matter, and as I have a great many things to attend to, I feel that any further argument would simply be a waste of my time and yours."

With that, Datilda stood up and walked away from her out of the lounge toward the door without saying a word and looked at her with pity. Grace stood up and watched her leave, then she walked over to the large windows and stared out at her, thinking as she watched her making her way along the path toward the gates alone.

"Oh, Father . . . what can I do?" Grace asked, looking up at her father's portrait where it hung just above the fireplace. While Datilda was walking, she felt a little sharp pain in her chest. The taxi was outside the gate, waiting. The taxi driver noticed that there was something wrong. He got out the taxi and walked up quickly toward her to help her back to the car.

"My god!" he exclaimed. Datilda was clutching herself. Her face changed colour.

"What's wrong? Are you all right?" the taxi driver exclaimed again as he bent over her before going back in his driver's seat. "Datilda, what's wrong? You don't look well."

"My chest . . . There's pain in my chest. My arm hurt. I think I'm having a heart attack."

"Don't try to move! I'll get you to the hospital. There's one not far away. I'll have us there in a few minutes."

He helped her into the taxi, closed the door, and drove off along the road. While driving, he looked into his mirror and again asked if she was feeling all right. She then responded, "Please stop off at the Blue Beard Hotel and ask for my granddaughter, Drusilla Becker, please!"

"Yes, Mama," he said, showing respect to their older generation.

As they approached the hotel, he got out and ran to the doors to the reception, asking for her granddaughter. About fifteen minutes later, Drusilla and the taxi driver walked out of the hotel and rushed over to the taxi, finding her grandmother not looking too well.

"What's wrong with my grandma?"

"Your grandmother has had a heart attack. Please come, we've got to go!"

The taxi driver, being worried to asked if he could help them, she told him to take them to the General Columbus Hospital, which was not far from where they were. Drusilla went into the taxi, and he drove them off to the hospital. In the taxi, Drusilla leaned over to shield her from the glare of the sun and asked, worried, "Are you in a lot of pain?" She wanted to put her arm around her. "Where were you going in a taxi?" The taxi driver was about to tell her when he looked at Datilda eyes in the mirror and saw that she didn't want her to know. She gave him a small wink of an eye, so he kept his mouth closed and continued to drive, praying all the way.

"Try not to worry, Grandma. You're going to be all right," Drusilla said as she fastened the seat belt around her, praying that she would be.

Datilda stared through the taxi windows at cars passing by, old trucks and people. The taxi driver then said, coming to a standstill outside the hospital emergency entrance, "This is it." Drusilla quickly paid the driver before getting out of the vehicle. Datilda emerged on the other side where the two paramedics brought a wheelchair and placed it near the taxi door for her to sit in. Drusilla went to make a phone call. While on the phone, her hands were shaking.

Leon was resting on his bed after some house duties when the phone rang. "Grandpa," Gracelyn called out.

He woke up and answered, "What is it, Gracelyn?"

"My mama is on the phone."

He heard Drusilla's soft voice. The voice started talking, "Paps, this is Drusilla."

"Hello . . . hello."

Paps!" She sounds as if she'd been crying.

"Yes. What? What time is it? What's up? What's wrong? Is everything okay?" he asked with his eyes protesting against the bright light coming from the window.

"No . . . No, it's not. Grandma isn't well."

He did not understand half of the words she said.

"Where is she?" he asked, terrified.

"She's in the hospital."

"Hospital!" he exclaimed. "Which hospital?"

"The General Columbus Hospital."

"I'll be there. I'm on my way."

He hung up the phone before she could take her next breath, and without thinking, he threw on a pair of trousers and a shirt, rushing outside, looking for Coretta, telling her to go with him, Glenn ran over to his father, asking what's wrong. Leon told him to inform the rest of the family that their grandmother was in the General Columbus Hospital and went on his way there. About half an hour later, he arrived at the hospital. He spoke to Drusilla and asked, "What's going on?" "So?" he asked again, being impatient and anxious to know.

As they were walking along the corridor, Leon's stomach sank. He was trembling, nervous for what to come next. The doctor walked up to Leon, Coretta, and the rest of the family and told them to follow him in one of the rooms along the corridor that were closed only by a curtain. "As a cardiologist," he said, "I recognized the pain in her chest as a heart attack." Datilda was placed on a hospital bed where Drusilla was questioned about the pains she was having, but first, the doctor read her card that contained all the information that they collected. Drusilla explained she felt a sharp pain.

"Where?" asked the doctor.

"In her chest, and her left arm hurts."

"Don't add anything else. She'll spend a night here."

He leaned toward Datilda and put a hand on her chest, working his way around the body, asking more questions of any previous pains coming from her chest. After some time, the pain eased, and the doctor managed to ask her questions.

"Does it hurt here?"

She said, "Sometimes."

"And here?"

"No."

The nurse went across the room to prepare the needle. The doctor asked Leon to walk with him. Drawing him to one side of the waiting room, he said, "Your mother has had a heart attack. Fortunately, not too severe."

"Please, Doctor, tell me, is she going to be okay?"

"She's going to be all right, but she will have to stay so we can see how she is."

"Yes, I understand, Dr. Baxter. How long will she have to stay in the hospital?"

"Is there nothing that we can do?" Coretta asked.

"A few days, five at the most. She's in our cardiac care unit, more for observation and a rest than anything else."

A few minutes later, the doctor walked into the room and glanced at Drusilla, who was lying on the bed near the window. A moment later, Leon was by the bed where Datilda lay, looking pale and weak.

"I'm sorry to put you all through this trouble," Datilda said in a low voice.

"Don't be silly," Drusilla exclaimed. "You're not any trouble for us, Grandma. Sheena and I are going to come and see you every day."

After receiving the news, Sheena went to the hospital. She approached the reception, asking for her grandmother by name. As the receptionist was speaking to several people, a doctor could not help but overhear while standing next to her. She did not respond because she was tired after some visits to patients. Then she responded by telling her that the rest of the family were there and that she would take her there. They took the lift. The lift doors slid open, and they both entered as they reached the floor where she was staying. They got out the lift and started to walk down the long hallway—248, 249, 250, 251, and, finally, her room, 252. The doctor opened the door, and Sheena entered the room while the others were leaving. The room was quiet; only the machine was on, reading Datilda's heartbeat. Datilda lay quietly in her bed, sleeping most of the time, and her breath was coming in gasps. Later in the evening, the family came to join Leon at the hospital. Sheena arrived and sat at the bedside with her chair overlooking her grandma so her face was right in front of hers. She was just looking at her, waiting for her to wake up.

"I'm a bit worried about Grandma because she is lying so quiet and still," said Sheena.

Leon went over to his mother's side. In an experienced manner, he placed his hand on her forehead. Drusilla smiled at her Grandma. The doctor walked in and called out to Sheena.

"You can sleep here with her if you want."

"Thank you," Leon murmured. "I don't know how to thank you."

"Thanks are not necessary. We will just leave her to rest."

"Thank you! Thank you so much," said Leon, shaking Dr. Baxter's hands, and left walking back to where his mother was lying. Finally, the shades opened, and the nurse walked out with a smile and placed a hand on Leon's shoulder as she was leaving. "Later, they will give her something."

An hour later, a nurse entered the room, asking them all to leave. Glenn then responded, "I think we all have had enough excitement for the day."

"Everybody, I think we should just go home now," Leon said.

Sheena went daily to the hospital to visit her grandma, just watching her sleep. Sheena tried not to sleep. She was too afraid of all the things that could go wrong. A monitor that showed her heart rate beeped next to her bed. The sheet tucked up under her chin.

She looked a little pale, but the nurse who came on regular visits told her that it was not unusual after a heart attack. The nurse, as gently as possible, bathed Datilda's entire body from head to toe with a sponge before the doctor came into the room to take blood samples.

"Don't worry, she's through the worst of it," the nurse said, rubbing her hand over Sheena's back.

Speaking to her grandma, Sheena said, "I know you are very ill and may not have long to live. I love you, and I want to tell you, *thank you* for being around. All wouldn't be possible if it weren't for you." Just then, Leon and Coretta arrived and entered the room.

"Don't make noise. She is still sleeping."

"Are you okay, honey?"

"Yes."

Datilda finally woke up, opening her eyes. She was very weak to move an arm with extreme difficulties. She turned to Sheena and smiled; she thought she would never see anything so pleasing to her.

"Sheena," she whispered.

"Grandma," she said with a smile.

"I heard your voice. I'm still here. It's not my time. Besides, I have two more things to do before I go," she whispered.

She asked to be alone with her granddaughter. Coretta and Leon headed out the room, leaving Sheena solely with her.

"Sheena, I must tell you something, but you must come back alone with Jonathan because it's something important . . . important that you both should know before I die."

"You're not dying."

"I am, and you know I am."

Datilda knew it was time to reveal her secret she had hidden for years from her family. She told Sheena to take the shoe box that she hidden. The past has a way of reaching into the present. Sheena's and Jonathan's life came into question, and only Datilda could help them see why these two families hate each other so much. It wasn't quite what it seemed to them.

"You must come back tomorrow early morning," she requested. "Okay, but don't forget you must come back with Jonathan and a shoe box hidden at the back of my drawer in my room. Don't tell anyone in the family."

"Okay!" She leaned over her face and kissed her on her forehead.

The following day, while the family was busy with their chores, Sheena went into Datilda's room. She found the box placed at the back of the drawer, like she said, and stared at it for a long time before she took it. Then the next day, while the family was busy with their chores and Datilda was sleeping, Sheena, from the hallway called Jonathan to join her at the hospital. She placed the shoe box into her bag and walked out. On her way to the hospital, she stopped by a flower shop, "May I help you?" an assistant asked.

"Yes, I'd like some flowers. It's for my grandma."

The clerk handed her the flowers with a get-well card. Sheena took the card and scribbled something on it; then she turned and thanked her. Soon after she walked to the information desk in the hospital lobby. "I have some flowers here for my grandma, Mrs. Shawn.

The receptionist looked at her and said, "I can have them delivered to her room for you."

"Sorry," Sheena said, "I want to take it to her myself. She's my grandma."

"All right." Sheena took the lift and pressed the button. The lift arrived. Sheena stepped out and began to walk along the corridor to Datilda's room. Sheena took the flowers and placed them in the vase and sat down on a chair next to the bed, staring at Datilda, wondering what she has to say. As Jonathan arrived, Datilda's eyes opened.

"Good morning, Grandma. Have you had breakfast, or would you like some tea?"

"I have had breakfast, child," Datilda answered. "And I want nothing except to talk to you both, so listen to me carefully."

Sheena and Jonathan sat down with the shoe box in her hands. Sheena breathes and lifts the lid that contained a packet of letters carefully tied with string. Datilda began, "What I'm about to show you isn't easy, but listen to me . . . it's important. You are the only ones in the world who I am sharing my secret. I have kept this secret all my life, but I feel now that it's time you both should know. Now what you are about to read are letters from your grandfather, Jonathan. These letters will help you both understand why our families are at war with each other."

She held them in front of her, wondering what was written. She took one of the letters. It was not long; it covered only the front side of the paper. She held the letter, sitting close by the bed with Jonathan alongside her and began to read.

June, 1930

Datilda, my love, I know when you read this letter, it will be too late, but I want very much to write you. I have been thinking of you almost constantly the past few weeks. I know I have broken your heart; it is very hard for me to write this letter. I am always so lost for words when it comes to you. I think you should be the first to know that Lucille and I are to be married within six months. I adore you. You are a wonderful person. Not only are you beautiful on the inside, but you are definitely beautiful outside as well. Everything about you is extraordinarily beautiful. Never did I imagine that I would ever meet someone like you. Being young and immature, I made a lot of mistakes. I just wish there was another way that we could be together, but there is not. You show the true meaning of how a man should treat a woman. No other woman has loved me like you. My life will forever be incomplete without you. You feared that I never loved you. I know it does not make any earthly sense now, but I do regret that I never had the courage to tell you deeply how much you really meant to me. The longer I have known you, the more have I loved from the deepest part of my heart. I love all that you are and will be. I will not forget you.

Charles T. Samson

As they read, their expressions changed, looking at one another. Sheena and Jonathan sat in silence for a long time, holding the letter. When she finished, Jonathan took the letter from Sheena's hand, folded it cautiously, slipped it back into the envelope, and carefully placed it among the other letters in the shoe box as she had removed them. Along with the letters was a locket. Sheena took the locket and opened it to reveal a melody so soft and sweet. Datilda was moved by its melody that reminded her of the times she and Charles spent together. She was snapped from the memories when Sheena closed the beautiful locket and placed it back among the letters in the shoe box.

In the shoe box, there were 172 letters, which Charles Samson had written, one per month, which no one else saw or read. He turned and looked at Sheena, saying, "My grandfather was in love with your grandmother, and my father knew it. I don't think my grandfather couldn't help falling in love with her, just like how I can't help loving you."

"It's a long story," she began.

"Apparently, there is this noble tradition of marrying within a certain class and colour. That's why my grandfather didn't marry her because she came from a family of farmers, and that's why he married Lucilla Walters, my grandmother." He continued, "It is not the past that we should be worried about; it is our future. Back in Seattle, Alan, my best friend, asked me *what were my feelings for you?* Before, when I was here on the island, I didn't actually thought about committing myself to someone seriously. I thought I knew what I really wanted until I went back to Seattle, and only then I knew. As written in my letter, you have given me every reason to fight. What my grandfather did then was unacceptable, but I understand it was a different time, but I will fight for our love."

Datilda called Jonathan to her and held his hand, "You're like your grandfather. He was a good man. You'll have a big fight ahead of you both, and it won't be easy. As long as I am here, I will help with my son, and you, Jonathan, your mother."

"Why my mother?" asked Jonathan.

"If she joins your side, then your father eventually will give in."

"You alone cannot fight against him, you will lose, and only regrets will remain like your grandfather."

"You loved him, didn't you?" asked Jonathan.

"Yes, but . . . ," responded Datilda, "what's important now is your future."

CHAPTER THIRTEEN

*T*he following morning, as usual, there were visits in each room to see how each patient was. Later in the afternoon, some of the family and friends came by to see her. A nurse came in the room, asking them to leave. Datilda called the nurse. She told her to write a letter to her son for her and that it must be sent after she had gone. The nurse left the room and returned with a notepad and began to write. Late in the evening, Jonathan walked past, not entering the room. He saw Sheena sitting on one side of her grandma's bed, holding her hand tight. Datilda opened her eyes and turned to where Jonathan was standing in the doorway; she looked at him with her radiant face and smiled with knowing eyes. He could tell she had welcomed her death and was allowing her family time to accept it too in their own time and way. Sheena slept close to her grandmother that night. When she woke up the following morning, Datilda was still sleeping. Sheena gently tapped her shoulders.

"Grandma," she repeated.

Still no answer. Datilda's face looked different as usual, and her eyes were loosely shut as if she was almost ready to wake up. Sheena touched her hand. It was cold and stiff. "Oh my god!" she screamed out crying, pressing her hands to her face. "Grandma! Grandma!" Sheena said, trying to wake her up, but there was no response.

"Grandma!" screamed Sheena crying. A nurse ran into the room, holding back Sheena. "She is not breathing." She ran out the room, looking for a doctor. A nurse-call signal was sent. It had immediately alerted the doctor. In a few hours, the room had been transformed into a hive of doctors. There was no hope; Datilda had died. Sheena stood above her grandmother, crying almost uncontrollably. Her pain was deep. She placed her hand upon hers and just felt tears run down her face. She sat down for a long time, weeping with her hands over her mouth. Jonathan had just arrived; he was outside the room in the hallway, waiting. He saw Sheena crying. He walked over to her and put his arms around her shoulders. Jonathan looked at her while the tears streamed down her face. "Are you okay?" he asked. "I'm so sorry."

"She's never coming back. She's gone," said Sheena sadly. She left us before we could tell her that she was right," she said as she continued to weep.

"She knew all along that her time would come," said Jonathan.

Suddenly, her head began to spin, and her knees were unsteady.

"Let me take you home," he offered.

She nodded and took his arm as they walked. There was a phone call from the hospital. The phone rang; Drusilla answered.

"Hello!"

"Hello, this is Dr. Baxter speaking."

"What's wrong?" Drusilla asked.

"I'm afraid it's not good news. Please tell your father, Mr. Becker, to come to the hospital as fast as he can," he said.

"Why, what's wrong?" again, Drusilla asked.

"It's his mother, she died."

Drusilla placed the phone on the table and rushed outside to call her father.

"Paps!" crying Drusilla.

"Hey, what's wrong?"

"Grandma's dead."

Leon dropped everything that was in his hand and ran quickly to the house to change. About half an hour later, Leon, Coretta, and the rest of the family arrived. Sheena left Jonathan and hugged her brothers as they went in the room. You could hear the whole family crying for the person they had most dearly loved passed away. Nothing can prepare you when death knocks on the door. Jonathan and Sheena left the hospital and headed home.

"I wanted her to look her best as she could," said the nurse.

"I will be just outside. You take as long as you like," said the nurse. Leon nodded his head and slowly walked in the room where his mother lay.

"I am sorry, honey. We knew this day would come," said Coretta, rubbing her hand on his shoulder.

"I just need to be alone with her for a while," said Leon as he closed the door.

Later, the door opened, and Leon called the rest of his family to join him. They stood all around the bed, holding each other's hands in silence, lowering their heads in prayer in silence to their heavenly father with tears running down their faces. As the door opened, the nurse knocked and entered the room, saying, "I am sorry, Mr. Becker, but it's time."

"Okay . . . She was a God-fearing mother, you know. She lived a good life."

"Your mother was a real woman. She left in a dignified manner. We all knew her," said the nurse.

Tears slide down his cheek while leaving the room.

"She died, and our lives will never be de same," Leon murmured, his face ringed with sorrow.

"But we must go on, that's what she would have wanted," said Coretta.

"Paps!" Sheena cried as she rushed forward into his arms.

For Sheena, it was difficult to return home, accepting the fact that her grandmother was gone. Leon held her tightly. His throat tightened, and for a moment, he could not speak.

Jonathan entered his house and asked for his mother. The maid, Charlotte, told him that she was in the garden, cutting her roses. Jonathan went up to his grandfather's bedroom, which was always closed after his death. As he unlocked the door, he saw that everything was just the same way it was when he was alive. Under the window was a leather-top kneehole desk; he looked out the window and saw his mother in the garden. He began to look in all the drawers and found nothing, just a fountain pen, an antique pocket watch, and a lion letter opener. While searching, it came to his mind to take the drawers out and look underneath them, hoping to find something hidden from his family. On his left side, on the second drawer up, he found something. This covered a sealed envelope. He took it from underneath, opened it, and began to read. The letter explained everything. He realized from the letter that it was not going to be easy for him to convince his father. At that moment, his mother entered the room and was surprisingly shocked to see him in the room with the drawers on the floor.

"Jonathan! What . . . what are you doing? This is outrageous."

"Look, Mother, look what I've found. All these years it's been hidden under our noses."

"This was your grandfather's room!" she responded angrily.

"I know, but look!"

"What will your father say when he gets back?" she said. "Do you know what you've done?"

"Mother, this is more important. Read it!"

Jonathan took his mother's hand and led her to the bed and gave her the letter to read. "I want you," said Jonathan, "to embrace yourself, for what you are about to read has never been told by Grandfather." She looked at the letter. "I want you to read it carefully," he continued. Her face changed with complete astonishment while reading the letter. The letter contained *expressions of love* and were not known by any other members of the family. She lifted her head, looking at Jonathan.

"How did you know where to find this letter?" He began to explain to her all the secrets that were revealed up to the death of Datilda. Grace did not know what to say or think; she was lost for words. Jonathan took the letter from his mother's hand. "No, Jonathan, I need to show it to your father. He has the right to see it," she said, trying to take it back, but Jonathan took hold of it while he was arranging the drawers back into place then closed the door behind them.

While walking down the hallway, Jonathan began to say, "Mother, this war must stop. It has been going on just far too long, and I don't want no part of it." Grace looked at him still shocked by the letter. "I have no intention of giving Sheena up. I love her, and I will fight for her," he continued.

He drew strength from his grandfather and Datilda's example, a touching portrait of a story between them unrevealed and fought for.

The following morning, Leon, together with his wife, was making the funeral arrangements.

They returned to the hospital to prepare what was needed to be done for his mother. As they were leaving, Dr. Baxter called out to Leon, "Mr. Becker?"

"Yes."

"I have a letter for you. Your mother asked me to give it to you while she was alive."

Leon stared at it as the doctor handed it over. He walked away, leaving him to open and read the letter. Coretta, watching him carefully, said softly, "Perhaps you would like to be alone when you read it."

"No," Leon said, "it's all right."

He opened the envelope and took out the letter and began to read.

To my son,

By the time you have read this letter, I have already left you all. This is my last letter. My spirit flies accompanied by all the happiness you have all given me. This time, I will not be with you to answer all your questions. I will be buried alongside your father, whom I love, and you will see us again promised by our heavenly father, as promised in 1 Corinthians 15:20-22. There is another thing you need to know. Jonathan Samson is a good young man. You must listen to him. I was seventeen when I met and fell in love with his grandfather. Go to your daughter, Sheena, and ask her for a shoe box. In there are letters that I kept all these years. Read them all, and you will understand why Jonathan's father has hated our family so much before you were born and long before I met your father, who knew all the story. I'm sorry I didn't mean for all this trouble to come to this. I didn't intend to hide my secrets. I didn't mean all of this would come to hurt the family. Can you forgive me? I pray and hope that you will find peace among you all and give your blessings to them with your whole heart as I have. And try to give attention to your daughter because she loves you and needs you more than ever.

Datilda, your loving mother

It was evening. Sheena was in her room, crying. There were noises of cars parking and doors closing. The rest of the family had returned from the hospital along with friends. Leon went into the lounge and embraced one another. He walked slowly up stairs toward Sheena's bedroom door and knocked.

"Can I come in, Sheena?"

"Yes, Paps," she said, wiping away the tears from her eyes.

"Hi, sweetie."

"Paps, she's gone."

"Yes, I know . . . We all miss her," he said with a sad low voice.

"I miss her, Papa," She said, embracing her father. "I miss her so much. I miss her hugs and affection."

Datilda's death was the most devastated experience that anyone could bear. She was a much-loved person. Sometimes the pain seems unbearable.

"I miss her too, honey."

"I feel totally alone and lost," said Sheena. "My grandma was my best friend. We spent a lot of time together."

"Sheena, I know it's not the right time, but she left me a letter and told me to ask for a shoe box," Leon said, standing in the doorway. "Do you have this box?"

"Yes. Why?" she asked. "You're not going to destroy them?"

"No, I must read them."

In the meantime, Coretta entered too in the room when Sheena was giving the box to her father.

"When I have finished reading them, I will give them back to you."

He walked out with the shoe box in his hand and went into his room alone. As he was about to open one of the last letters, his wife knocked and walked in the room. Leon gave her one of the letters to read; she was astonished of a love story between his mother and Charles Samson.

"Your mother knew all along that the Samson family would never accept our daughter. She knew they would never admit that our daughter was acceptable for their son. But what I don't understand is why he hates us so much."

"Didn't you read the rest of it?" he said with shock. "He hates our family because my mother had affection for your father. They were both passionately in love. He blames her for the death of his mother."

"But how can your mother be the cause of her death?"

"I don't know, but ever since then, it seems like there's been a never ending argument between our families."

"And now," asked Coretta.

"I don't know," responded Leon.

"Well, I think you need to talk with Jonathan. Now is the right time," responded Coretta.

"He's a Samson too!"

"Yes, but he is in love with our daughter. Just listen to what he has to say." She could see the hurt in his eyes.

Four days later, Sheena's parents arranged her funeral. Datilda's body was taken to Mere Wood Cemetery, where she was laid beside her beloved husband. The Becker family and other family members stood near the grave. Behind them were people from a nearby village, and those who knew her in town came to pay their respects.

CHAPTER FOURTEEN

*B*y now, darkness had come. The stars were shining in the sky, and the moon was rising slowly above the trees. There was no one to hear Jonathan or see him as he walked under Sheena's bedroom window. He knew that the family would by now be comfortably asleep. He could see that there was no light behind the curtains. He whistled, and there was no response. Sheena heard a noise. She thought it was just her imagination. He whistled repeatedly, and there was no response. He then threw pebbles against the window. She woke up, went to the window and drew the curtains back, and looked out. Sheena leaned out of the window to see who it was. She saw it was Jonathan standing outside her window.

"What are you doing here?" she whispered with surprise.

"I must see you!" Jonathan said in a low voice to her.

Sheena nodded and pointed with her finger below her to the left, where he saw there was a door. He nodded to show that he understood and moved toward it. She went back into the room, putting on her dressing gown. She hesitated for a moment, wondering if it would be wise to keep Jonathan waiting. Somebody might be aware that he was there. She heard her father go to bed about an hour ago. She did not want to take any chances, so she blew the candle out, opened her door quietly, stepped onto the landing, and pressed her ear to the door to hear her father's soft snores and smiled, then she tiptoed barefoot along the corridor quickly and quietly down the stairs toward the kitchen door. He was standing just outside. Before she could get the door completely opened, he swept her into his arms. She was everything he wanted and which he swore he would never lose.

"I had to come. I missed you!" he said, kissing her. "I know how you feel. Your grandmother was a good person," he said.

Drusilla woke to the sound of voices coming from outside her window. She cleared her eyes and walked toward it and glimpsed behind her curtains and saw Jonathan outside, talking to Sheena. She walked out of her room, went down the stairs, and waited in the lounge. Drusilla, the eldest sister, worked in a hotel where she was underpaid, which did not allow her to put aside her savings. The garden door closed, and Sheena walked barefoot passing the lounge. Drusilla called her in an ascus phonetic transcription low voice, "Sheena!"

Drusilla's voice made her jump.

"Oh, you scared me. Why are you up at this time?" Sheena asked.

She walked to the lounge, where Drusilla was without looking back.

"I heard noises out the window, and I saw it was Jonathan and you," she said. "If Paps was to catch you . . . you know what will happen."

"I know, you will not believe me, but if I cannot be with him, I shall never love anyone else in the same way as I love Jonathan!"

As she spoke, Drusilla understood that Sheena was suffering in a way that she had never experienced. She was very young and so lighthearted to suffer. Drusilla was worried for her sister. It frightened her that as she said *she would never love anybody else in the same way*, and there was a pause. Drusilla did not reply. Sheena turned and went up the stairs. Her head was bowed, walking very differently. She sighed. Drusilla made certain the garden door was locked and went up the stairs to her own room. She felt almost as depressed as Sheena.

"I hate the Samson family for what they are doing to my sister!" she told herself angrily, but at the same time, she knew that Jonathan was different from the rest of his family.

Soon after dinner, Grace said she was leaving her husband in the lounge to go to bed early. She went up the stairs, wondering what she could say to him. As she began to undress herself for bed, she found herself thinking that, although she dared to admit it, Sheena and Jonathan were well suited to each other. She knew her husband would never admit that. While entering the room,

Steven heard a noise. He walked out on the landing and found Jonathan climbing up the stairs to his room. He did not say a word or looked before he closed the door. Steven re-entered his room again when Grace walked over to him to talk about their relationship and a letter that Jonathan found in his father's room and that she too had read. Steven stopped undressing, turned to Grace, and began to say, "I don't care what he has found. He is not going to have his way. He's already twisting you around his little finger."

"I am sorry, darling, that's not true, and you know it. It's just that I am worried about all this. It has been going on for many years, and I don't know why it has to continue even for the future of our son," Grace said. "Why make Jonathan more unhappy? We can't live our existence on revenge. These people are not our enemies!" she continued.

"Do you have this letter?"

"No, Jonathan has it," she said.

"Will you do what I tell you?"

Grace hesitated and said for the first time in their married life, "I'm not sure, Steven. What are you saying?"

"Meet her and try if you can persuade her to stop seeing our son."

"I'll do no such thing," Grace said angrily. "What's happening to us?"

"I don't know what you mean, Grace."

"We're drifting apart with all these problems and work."

"Don't be silly!" he exclaimed. "Our life is very much on track."

"It's no marriage. You have a career you love, but your family, our son, you have neglected!"

"I don't understand."

"We're never together. We are always in different places here on the island and Seattle, and when we're at home, you haven't got a lot to say to me anymore, and another thing, we don't seem to be close physically as we were."

Shaking his head, he threw his tie on the chair and walked over to her, pulling her to sit down on the bed next to him. "Grace, I love you, you know that. Nothing's changed between us. Well,

I'm successful, very successful, that's true, and I'm happy. Everything now is for our future, yours and mine, our old age."

"Old age!" she exploded. "I want to live now while I'm young, with my husband and son."

"We are living, and living very well." He looked deeply into her eyes and said softly, "I guess I have been neglecting you lately. I'm sorry." He put his arms around her and kissed her. "We are going to Seattle to pay a visit to a doctor."

"Why? Are you ill?" she asked worried.

"No, it's Dr. Benjamin Wilkinson that treated my mother. I must know the truth. I need to know," he said as he places his shirt on an iron and trouser presser. "I don't want to talk about it now. Let's get some sleep. It's late." They got into bed and switched of the bedside lamp. Steven's eyes were kept open, thinking about the letter.

The following morning, Steven had a business meeting with a few business clients from New York and London. That same morning, Sheena was in the market, helping her mother set up her stall. Sheena told her mother she was going to meet her friends in town, so they would go to university together. So as she walked away from the market, she was about to cross the street, not knowing that Steven Samson saw her. He turned into a car park and pulled into a parking space. The car stopped. Dozens of large boxes were scattered around near a supermarket on the other side of the road. Steven got out of his car and began to follow her on foot. At a moment, Sheena walked into a bar. "Hi, everybody. I don't have time to chat. I must rush. I'm going to take some dumplings." She picked up several and covers them with paper napkins. "See you later," she said, leaving the money on the counter. As she crossed over the road, Sheena had a strange feeling that came over her that someone was behind her, following her. Steven called out to her. She turned, not knowing who it was. Steven held himself very stiff at Sheena with his fiery eyes, revealing who he was. He stared intensely with no secret of his disapproval and anger written across his face. This time, she was more mature, more knowledgeable and able to deal with the threats that she was about to face. "I'm not afraid of you," she said.

He took a large sniff, not that it really mattered since he would never look at her as anything more than a nobody before saying, "Then let me explain it to you, Ms. Becker. You are not going to see my son again. I want you to stop trying to persuade my son in marrying you and instead allow him to do as his family wishes if you want your brother to keep his job."

She blinked. "And what if that is not what he wishes?" Sheena asked.

"Do you have any idea how pathetic that makes you?"

"No, but it makes me strong. I know you dislike me," she said.

She was trying to keep her calm because she was so angry with Steven Samson for what he had said.

"I have not come here to quarrel or waste time with you," he said. "I am sure when I have the opportunity to speak to my son, he will do what I ask of him. After all, I don't think you can say you know him very long, Ms. Becker. He is aware of his responsibilities to his family."

"I would be very surprised if he becomes a puppet for you to pull the strings and do exactly what you want."

"Don't think that you will ever become a member of our family," he replied. "It will never happen."

Sheena was not at all inclined to surrender all she'd believed in. She watched him leave, walk toward his car, and drive off. *I am not going to let him frighten me*, she thought. She turned and walked away quickly. Even so, she was frightened.

That same evening, Sheena decided not to tell Jonathan that she met his father, for it could ruin their evening. Jonathan soon returned with Sheena to her house. Outside the front door, Sheena hesitated.

"You know it's not too late to cancel," Sheena said, worried.

"Why . . . why would we do that?" asked Jonathan, puzzled.

"I don't know," said Sheena, frowning. "It seems real, like we weren't meant to get to this stage," she continued.

"That's exactly why we're going to do it," said Jonathan with a smile on his face.

"Now?"

"Yes."

At that instant, she extended her hand to Jonathan, and he grasped it; then drawing her close, they both walked up to the front entrance of the house. Sheena came to a standstill in the lounge and then said, "Mama! Paps! I would like you to meet Jonathan. He wants to meet you officially, so please be nice to him. He is important to me." She went back to fetch him. As she returned, Jonathan was with her. "This is Jonathan." They both turned. Leon stood up from his seat, raised one eyebrow, stared at her for five seconds, and walked over to him offering his hand.

"Jonathan!"

Leon looked straight at him. "Mr. Becker." Jonathan shook his hand; he had a firm grip.

"Take a seat."

"I mean no disrespect, but since Sheena has already said yes after I have asked her hand, I'm begging you for your blessing. We're getting married. I love her more than anything in the world, and she chose me in the same way too. Will you give us your blessing?"

"You're joking, you can't be serious. She hardly knows you!"

"Enough, Paps!" Glenn said as he restrained his father's speech because he was getting agitated.

Leon paused and looked at them for a long time, studying them; then after the hesitation, he went on, "Are you sure?"

"Yes, I am," responded Sheena.

"I knew it would happen sooner or later . . . Okay, fine." He called his wife, "Coretta!"

"Yes."

"Come here!

"My little child, luckily, you seem to be all grown up."

"Then we must talk, and I want to apologize."

Sheena's father spoke in a calm seriousness.

"Would you like to stay and have dinner with us, Jonathan? We could get to know you better."

"Sure," he replied.

Dinner was ready (roast beef with a sherry-laced cream of mushroom gravy, curried lobster, scalloped potatoes, plantains wrapped in bacon, green salad, and staple rice and peas). All, except one, was sitting at the table as Leon made grace before eating. "Heavenly father, as we are here before you . . ."

Sheena sat there staring at the empty chair for a moment in silence, thinking as memories flashed through her mind of Datilda's soft voice. She felt a mix of emotions such as depression. At that moment, the room fell in silence. Jonathan noticed her expression of silence and asked cautiously, "You're quiet . . . Something wrong?"

She snapped out of it and responded, "No, I'm okay."

Then she stood up quickly from her seat and walked out on the terrace and cried silent tears. Jonathan joined her, embracing her with comfort and told her to accompany him with the rest of her family. She wiped her tears from her eyes before walking back into the lounge, where the rest of the family were without speaking. They all started talking again as if nothing happened. They sat down. "I have something for you." Jonathan took from his inside jacket pocket an envelope that was addressed to Datilda before she died. "I found this in my grandfather's room under his desk," he said, showing her the envelope. He began to read it out loud for them to hear. After he read, he began saying, "I know this is not the moment, but I think your mother, Mr. Becker, would have wanted all of you to know, after my grandfather died confessing in this letter, that he felt alone. The sunlight, your mother, Mr. Becker, as he calls her, had gone from his heart, and no amount of love Lucilla Walters, my grandmother, could give him would compensate the woman he really loved. He was forced to marry my grandmother for the sake of both families. Further on in this letter, he continued saying the cause of his wife's death was a brain disease, and she didn't have long to live, so she kept it a secret from everybody, only her doctor knew. The doctors were unable to control her illness with counseling and medicines alone, and only then she revealed her secret for the first time to my grandfather that she was dying. When my grandfather learnt of her illness, he decided to take her to a specialist who would diagnose her illness, but she refused. So now, here is the tragic part. When my grandmother decided to take her own life by committing suicide, she was found lying on the floor in her room. My grandfather was found kneeling down over her. It was easy for the Samsons to accuse the Becker family for her death, knowing the why she did it. So this is the reason all these years, our families are at war, and it's only now the truth has come out," Jonathan explained. They all looked at each other with shock and hate. Leon stared down at the envelope. *Datilda*, his grandfather had written across the front. He stared at it as Jonathan handed it to him.

Coretta interrupted Jonathan, "You must forgive me, Jonathan, if I interrupt you, but why did she keep her illness a secret from her own family? What was her reason?"

Jonathan could not answer. "Well, I don't know," He said, moving his head left to right. "I haven't read the entire letter. Maybe there is an explanation to that question and many more."

As it was getting late, Jonathan decided to get up and leave the family. Sheena followed him to the terrace. He turned to her with a smile on his face. "This wasn't how I imagine the evening would end. I thought it would end differently."

"Me too," Sheena admitted.

The following morning, back in Seattle, Steven and his wife decided to meet his mother's doctor, Dr. Benjamin Wilkinson. *[Nothing hurts like the truth. A truth that has haunted him all his life. A truth that has never been revealed to no one. Nevertheless, the truth is about to meet its greatest test.]* On his arrival in the clinic, behind a desk in the lobby was a receptionist who appeared to be in her forties.

"Good morning," Steven said.

The receptionist looked up at him. "Morning." Steven introduced himself to the woman behind the desk and explained that he had an appointment. "Oh yes, please follow me," she said. They followed the receptionist who was escorting them to the doctor's studio. She opened a wide door, and they walked in the room and closed the door behind them. Steven greeted Dr. Wilkinson with a handshake and told him to call him by his first name, Steven. He told them both to sit. Steven's eyes darted from side to side. Before questioning the doctor about the cause of his mother's death, including whether he would follow in his mother's footsteps, he could see there was a long couch against the wall behind him, and the other walls of the room were covered with shelves filled with books. Dr. Wilkinson gently explained that it was not genetical.

"Your mother's situation was far greater than she was willing to admit. Her frontal lobe was damaged. And the only ones who knew the truth were her and I. Eventually, your father who came to me to find out more about her illness," he continued. "This disease is more common among men. Very few women get it."

"What were the symptoms?"

Here the doctor began to explain, "Well, the brain is a soft, spongy organ made up of nerve cells and tissue. It is divided into three major sections: the cerebrum, the cerebellum, and the brainstem. The cerebrum is the largest part of the brain and is divided into two halves called the right and left hemispheres. The right hemisphere controls the left-hand side of the body, and the left hemisphere controls the right-hand side of the body. Each hemisphere is further divided into sections called lobes." He paused for a few seconds before he continue to explain. "There are four lobes in each hemisphere: the frontal, parietal, occipital, and temporal. The frontal lobe is responsible for attention, thought, reasoning, behaviour, movement, sense of smell, and sexual urges. A frontal lobe tumor can cause this inhibition by behavioural disturbance and poor judgment. There was nothing I or anyone else could do. I was responsible for her care. She continued her daily routine in the family, which was very important, but I told her to break the news to her husband, which she didn't. Here,"—he hands a copy of her file—"they are all the reports of her illness and visits before she died."

Steven took the reports and looked at them one by one; he was confused, "So the cause of her death was that she was dying not for the fact that she committed suicide?"

"Well, I think she took her own life for the fact that she couldn't stand the thought that she would suffer, so maybe she thought taking her own life would be easier. Yes, her formal lobe was damaged. I wasn't able to treat it. It was too late."

Again, Steven looked at the reports, still not accepting the fact of his mother's death. "My mother . . . I really don't think she was . . ." The doctor suggested some books for him to study on the basics of his mother's illness and rose from his seat, leaving them both in the room alone.

Grace placed her hand over Steven's hand, trying to show sympathy for his pain, and worried at the same time of his reaction to the truth being hidden from him from his childhood. As the doctor re-entered his studio, he heard a buzzing sound. He pushed a button, picked up the phone, nodded, then put the receiver back down. Steven and Grace then rose from their seats and walked to the door. As he opened it, the doctor muttered, "Have a nice day." Grace turned and said, "Thank you." Once out the doctor's studio, Steven's mind was so jumbled that he did not know how to react.

"No! No! No!" Steven yelled. "This can't be true. It's all lies. They've hidden the truth. I know they have."

"Dear, I saw the letter that your father wrote. It's true. There are no lies. Your mother was dying."

"My mother died committing suicide," he said, looking at the papers in his hand.

"How do you know? Who told you this?" she asked.

"No one, I was seven when she died. I was in the hallway, and I overheard my grandfather talking to someone, accusing the Becker family for her death."

"Did you know who was in the room with your grandfather?"

"No, I could only see my grandfather through the gap of the door. They were shouting at each other, and the last thing I heard was that my grandfather would make the Beckers pay for what they did. So I too grew to hate that family."

"What about your father? Did he say anything to you?"

"No! I could see he was sad but at the same time worried."

"Worried about what?" Grace asked.

"I don't know. I've never asked," Steven replied.

Steven felt more upset than he had before. After leaving the building, his Mercedes pulled up where they were standing. The chauffeur opened the car door for them. Grace got inside the car and sat in the backseat. Steven said, "You're beautiful. I don't know what I would do without you."

"Thank you, darling," she said with a smile on her face, placing her hand on his. "Let's go home."

The chauffeur closed the door behind him as he was entering the car, then the Mercedes started off. Before arriving at the airport, Steven told his driver to take them to the cemetery and to leave him there and take his wife back to the house. The car slowed for a moment only to shift into a lower gear. Grace looked at Steven as if she wanted to say something to make him feel better. He looked toward Grace with tears in his eyes. Grace had never seen him act like that before. He just could not accept it; he stayed glued by his side. The car began to slow down as they were approaching, and then it stopped just outside Mere Wood Cemetery, where both his parents were buried. This part of the cemetery was well kept. Walking up to the spot where his mother lay, he stopped for a moment to rub his eyes. He stared down at the grave, kneeled beside it, and placed a bunch of flowers over her grave. He missed her so; she was young and beautiful when she died. A tear began to trickle down on one side of his face. Searching for the truth is easy, but for Steven, accepting it was hard. A little soft breeze blew whispering through the grass and stroked the leaves upon the trees as he sat on a stone bench, facing his mother's tombstone, thinking for a moment, holding an envelope. He pulled her medical test results from it in his hand, reading them over and again. He stared and stared, trying to come to terms. "How is it possible?" he said to himself. "Why would anyone lie and keep it a secret for all those years? Why?" He rose from the stone bench, "Goodbye," said Steven softly, facing the headstone and silently walked away.

Soon, Jonathan's presence in Sheena's home was becoming more and more regular. Her family and Jonathan would all laugh over games after dinner and enjoy many discussions on topics of all kinds.

They quickly discovered that Jonathan was completely different from his father and was more like Sheena's father. That evening, before Jonathan left, Leon approached them both and stared at them for a long time. "Guess, I'd have to deal with this sooner or later. Are you sure about this, Sheena?" Leon demanded, glaring at her.

"Yes, Paps," she told him.

"Okay," he said, "you have my blessing."

Leon gave his complete and full blessing for their engagement. Jonathan and Sheena were happy to hear this news. They walked out together on the terrace, and Jonathan began to say, "I love you, Sheena." Then he kissed her. They both turned, looking up to the sky. That night, it was filled with stars.

"Look how beautiful the sky is," Sheena said.

"Like you!" Jonathan commented with a smile. "You're the most beautiful and important thing that has ever happened to me. I'm alive because of you, and I don't want only to see you and tell you how beautiful you are, but I also want to hold you in my arms and kiss you." Sheena smiled. Jonathan held her in his arms and continued, "What happened," he asked, "to the young woman who hoped she would never see me again?"

"She was taken captive, conquered, and is now your prisoner!" she responded with her soft voice.

As his lips touched hers, she said, smiling, "I told you that it was destiny, and it's no use saying it's not."

"Come with me," he said as he held her hand.

"Where are we going?"

"Somewhere quiet. We are to take these moments, Sheena, right? What my father is doing is not important because I want you. It's just you and me, Sheena, always." She smiled, gazing into his eyes. "It's just so nice to see you smile," Jonathan said as he stroked her hair with a touch so light that she could hardly feel it.

"It's not going to get any easier is it?" Sheena asked sadly.

"No, no, it's not," unhappily responded Jonathan.

"I want to give you something," Jonathan said. He pulled out from his trousers pocket a small wooden carved box with a bow. "I want you to have this," He said, holding it in his hand. Sheena was breathless.

"It's beautiful!" Sheena said, staring into the box.

"It's something I had, and I wanted to give it to someone very special to me."

It didn't seem possible that he could care so deeply for someone other than his mother, but he did. Sheena untied the bow and then lifted the lid off the box and gently took the necklace from the small box and, with Jonathan's help, placed the necklace around her neck.

"Oh, it's very beautiful!" she gasped in delight.

After placing the necklace around her neck, he kissed the softness of her neck before he added, "I love everything about you."

"I told you that our love was destiny," she said again. Then he kissed her not gently, but passionately. After, she reached out and took hold of his hand and held it tightly in hers.

CHAPTER FIFTEEN

*B*ack in Seattle, Alan decides to make a call to Steven in his office. "Alan, my boy . . . How are you?"

"Fine, Mr. Samson, business is going well here in Seattle. Listen, I am flying out tomorrow to see Jonathan. How is he, by the way?"

"Please call me, Steven. You're a member of the family. Well, I don't know if you have heard. It's not important at the moment. I and my wife, Grace, would be delighted to see you. I will pick you up at the airport."

"Okay." Alan smiled. "Tell Jonathan his so-called brother is coming."

"Okay!" Steven hung up the phone.

Alan took a direct flight to the island. His plane landed a day earlier from Seattle; it was raining a few drops. At the airport, Steven was waiting for him with his car. He only had a few bags.

"It's good to see you, Alan," he said, smiling as he embraced him. "Hope you had a safe journey. How's your mother?" Steven said, placing his hand on Alan's shoulder as they walked toward the car while the chauffeur took his luggage, placing it at the back of the boot.

"She's fine. I hope you don't mind me coming."

"No, not at all. I will fill you in with the details of what's been happening here on this island with Jonathan."

"I know all about it," Alan said. "I just don't understand why you don't approve of her."

As they reached the Samson mansion, Grace heard the car arriving and opened the door to greet them. She stood there on the steps at the front entrance of the house, smiling at them. She stretched out her hand. "Hello, Alan. Come on in." He followed her into the house and stood there glancing around. Grace said, "Give your bags to her. They will take them up to your room."

"Thank you," he said. "So where's my brother?"

"He's upstairs in his room," replied Grace. "I'll call him. Jonathan, dear, Alan's here," she called him with a soft voice.

"Here I am!" Jonathan said with a happy smile on his face, walking up to him with a huge hug.

Jonathan was glad his best friend took the opportunity to visit him on the island. They were exceptionally close and shared the same interests and understood each other well. Alan looked around. "I want to show you the house," Grace said. Everything was in the best of taste.

"What a place!" he exclaimed. It's beautiful. I'd like to own something like this one day." Steven joined them and took Alan up to his room.

"Go and get freshened up and join me in the lounge."

"Great, I will be down in a minute."

As Steven was leaving, Jonathan arrived.

"I'm glad you're here," Jonathan said, "but I'm sorry I must leave you. I'm going to see her."

"So when do I have the pleasure to meet the one who stole your heart?" he asked, teasing.

"Soon," answered Jonathan, placing his right hand on the wall near the entrance of the room.

"See you tomorrow morning."

After Alan had a shower, he had buttoned his white shirt, pulled on his trousers with his black pair of shoes, and went down the stairs. He found Steven sitting in the lounge alone with a glass of whisky in one hand with a cigar in the other. "Please, help yourself," he said, "and sit down."

He poured himself a glass and sat down. "I'm glad you're here, Alan," Steven said. "What you said earlier, I'm sorry"—he shook his head—"but I'm not taking it." His voice was suddenly low and unpleasant. "It's got to stop. I'm not kidding, and you're going to help me do it." Alan shook his head in disgust. "You don't want to be stuck in the same position all your life."

"Why me? He's my best friend. We grew up together. I can't do this to him . . . You're kidding, right?"

"You know, if you want something badly enough, you usually get it if you work hard at it, but in this case, you could gain more than what you're earning now. The deal is to find a way to break this so-called relationship."

"No, I don't want no part of it," he said seriously.

"If you want, it can come earlier, that is, if you know what I mean?"

"But . . ."

"But what? That's all there is to it. We don't really care, do we?" Steven said. "SO DO WE HAVE A DEAL?" he repeated. "I'm a man of my word. When I make a deal, I keep a deal."

"Yeah," he said as he gave Steven his hand. "We have a deal."

"Cheers," said Steven, clinking their glasses.

The following afternoon, as Jonathan and Alan were in a café in town, waiting for Sheena, only a few people were about. They were sipping their drinks quietly, lost for a moment in their own thoughts. Breaking the silence, Alan said, "When is she coming?" Jonathan was about to say something when a few minutes later, the door of the café opened. The two of them turned their heads and stood up, silently staring at each other. A woman came into the café along with a cool gust of air. Alan burst out, "My god! Jonathan." She was more attractive in person than in the photograph that was on Jonathan's desk in Seattle. Alan's mouth hung open. Jonathan walked up to greet her. She smiled as she walked toward them. Jonathan drew close and kissed her on the cheek.

"Hi, I'm Alan Cruz," Alan said, introducing himself, smiling warmly. "So this is the beauty queen that stole my brother's heart."

Jonathan nodded his head. "Yes, Sheena, this is my best friend, but we act as brothers because we have always been together since we were kids."

"Hi, I have heard highly about you. Jonathan has told me so much."

He could not keep his eyes off her. He was taken by her beauty, watching her take a seat. After some time, Sheena got up to greet some friends who were sitting at another table.

"Blow me down, Jonathan! Where did you find such beauty? I've never seen a woman so beautiful."

"I don't want to sound like a jealous boyfriend, but . . ."

"Well, you do," responded Alan. "Don't worry. I'm not going to do anything."

A few seconds later, she came back to where they were. She pushed her chair behind the table and said, "Excuse me for a moment," and left the table, heading for the ladies' room. Jonathan leaned over to Alan and said, "So what do you think of her?"

"She's beautiful!" Alan said, mesmerized by her beauty and irresistibility too.

As Alan was talking, Jonathan thought to himself how lucky he was to have found her. Alan stopped as Sheena was returning to the table. The two roused from their seats, and Jonathan helped Sheena into her chair. Once she was seated, she smiled at Jonathan and leaned back against him. Jonathan reached out and took hold of her hand, knowing better than to say a word. They sat in the café and had an ice cream topped with small delicious decorations, while she ordered sandwiches and a juice. Alan was enjoying being together, getting to know Sheena. After Alan got up and walked over to the counter, leaving Jonathan and Sheena talking.

"I like him," she said. "He's sincere. He really cares about you."

Jonathan looked at her. "Yes."

As evening drew in, Jonathan was in the shower when he heard the phone ringing. He did not pick it up to answer. Alan, walking pass Jonathan's room, heard the ringing tone. He called out to him, saying, "Jonathan, your phone is ringing."

Jonathan shouted from the shower, "Alan, answer it, please."

It was only a second or two before she heard Alan saying, "Hey!"

"Hi! Where's Jonathan?" Sheena asked.

"He's under the shower. I'm doing great, thank you for asking," joked Alan.

"I'm checking on Jonathan." Sheena smiled.

"Oh, him!" said Alan sarcastically.

"Why? What's the matter?" asked Sheena, worried as if something happened.

"He's singing in the shower."

"I have got to go. I'm late. Tell him I will meet him in the city at Ronald's." Then she hung up.

Jonathan stepped out of the shower, reached for a towel, partially dried himself, and put on his bath robe, tightening the belt. Walking into his room, he heard Alan's voice saying goodbye. Alan walked over to Jonathan and handed over his phone. "Sheena called," he said and walked out the room. Returning to the bathroom, he combed his wet hair and finished drying himself then went back to his room to get dressed, putting on blue jeans and a T-shirt. By that time, Alan had taken Steven's car keys and went ahead with the plan, helping Steven show his son see who Sheena really was. He drove to the city, hoping to find her there. He could see Sheena talking to a group of girlfriends. He walked over to where she was. She whirled around when she heard someone behind her. He was dressed in his creamy suit and blue shirt as she had first seen him.

"Hi!" Sheena.

"Hi! Alan, you're alone. Where's Jonathan?" she asked.

"He couldn't come. He told me to break the news to you."

"Oh, that's strange. He should have called. He usually does."

"Well, maybe because of all that you are both going through, it just slipped his mind."

"Well, err . . . ," she said. "I'll better go home then."

"If you want, I'll take you."

"I have my car not far from here."

"Then I'll walk with you to the car."

"Okay, thank you."

As they were walking and talking, Alan moved closer to her that his clothes brushed hers and began to flirt.

"You look nervous."

"That's probably because I am."

"Well, Sheena, you're beautiful," he said stepping closer. "I understand why Jonathan is in love with you, but do you think all of this is worth fighting for? Jonathan is an idiot to think he will win."

Sheena looked at Alan. "You're his best friend. How could you do this to him? He loves you as a brother!" said Sheena.

"Face the truth, Sheena. Don't you be as stupid as he is," he said. "His father will never give up, and I know Jonathan. He will leave you eventually at the end, but this time, it will be for good. Accept things the way they are now. They're not the same as they once were. They haven't been for a long time."

The smile on her face dropped as he continued.

"Don't worry. I'm willing to take his place," Alan said, running his fingertips down her arm. Sheena pulled away and slapped him. She looked straight at him.

"What do you want? You disgust me," she exclaimed. "I have already found who I want to be with." She had not thought of doing it before she did it, and after, she could not believe what she had done. However, it was a good hard slap with the full strength of her body, and it moved Alan's head to one side.

"Where's Jonathan? And don't lie to me!" she said angrily.

"I know what you want." Alan smiled.

"I'm warning you, if you hurt me . . ."

"Then what?" he said. "What will you do, Sheena? What can you do against me?"

Sheena fell silent and quickly walked away toward her car, leaving Alan behind, not glancing back to see if he was following her. As she got home, she ran up to her room. When her phone rang, it was Jonathan.

"Hello?"

"Hi. It's Jonathan, Sheena. I missed your call."

"Did you get my call?"

"No, I didn't. I was in the shower when you called."

"Can you come over?"

"I can't!"

"I need to talk to you about something, not on the phone."

"Tell me what it is."

"It's really urgent."

There was something in her voice that made him suspicious that something had happened. He agreed. "All right."

In the meantime, Kirk was in the kitchen, making himself a corned beef sandwich. He opened the fridge door and took out a cold beer. After swallowing a few gulps, he went into the lounge, carrying a plate with his sandwich. He sat down and switched on the television, changing from channel to channel. He ate his sandwich and drank his beer, staring at the TV. He leaned back, taking occasional swallows of his beer. After a moment, his eyes began to feel heavy. He switched off the TV, put the plate and beer on the small glass coffee table, and curled up in the sofa and drifted off to sleep. As Jonathan set off for Sheena's house, which was on the other side of the island, it would have taken him about an hour-and-a-half drive to get there. Since there was no heavy traffic, he arrived an hour early. Jonathan stopped and parked his car in the yard, got out, and walked up toward the front door and knocked on the door. There was no answer. He knocked again and waited. Kirk awoke to a knocking sound coming from the front door. He felt disoriented after a nap. He blinked as he looked around the room. In the distance, the sound that awakened him continued. He cleared his eyes, got up on his feet, and crossed the room to the window. Jonathan was standing on the pavement outside. He quickly shouted, "I'm coming!" and flung open the front door with one eye closed to find himself facing Jonathan, standing there.

"Hi, Jonathan."

"Hi, Kirk," he said, coming in.

"What time is it?" he asked, finally able to open his eyes fully.

"Four."

"Four? I'm late."

"Is Sheena in?" asked Jonathan.

"Yes."

Kirk yelled out, "Sheena, Jonathan's here!"

"Okay. I'll be right down."

"I can't believe it. I'm late," Kirk said to himself.

"Late for what?" Jonathan stood watching as he put things in order.

"For work!" shouted out Kirk as he was running up the stairs to his room.

Sheena did not know what to do. She looked in the mirror and grimaced at herself. She looked dreadful, with mascara running down her face and red bloodshot eyes. She quickly washed her face and walked out, closing the door behind her. Before going down, she saw Kirk on his bed rolling a cigarette. Kirk stared at her. It was obvious that his sister had been crying, but Kirk thought it was better not to say anything. She walked past his room and went down the stairs. As soon as Sheena saw Jonathan, she hugged him tightly for a minute, then she said, "Hi!"

"Hi! You called while I was in the shower. What's up?" he asked.

"Nothing," she said.

Suddenly, Jonathan became aware of Sheena's troubled face and bloodshot eyes as if she had been crying something had upset her feelings. Her whole body was shaking in his arms; he was concerned.

"Sheena, what's wrong?"

"Come with me," She said, leading him to her room.

After Sheena sat on the edge of the bed, Jonathan stood, staring down at her and began to ask. "Hey, what's wrong?" he whispered. "Please tell me what's bothering you."

Jonathan, staring intently at her, realized something was wrong. Tears flooded her eyes, and she clasped her hands together to stop them from trembling. Jonathan was about to ask her again what was causing her to be upset when Sheena cleared her throat, reached out, and took Jonathan's hand. Sheena said slowly, "I have been trying to reach you on the phone."

"I was under the shower," Jonathan explained.

Her eyes moistening, as she lowered her face, her shoulders shaking…She slowly raised her head, tears rolling down her cheeks. "It's Alan!"

Sheena continued to cry. Jonathan sat next to her on the edge of the bed, put his arm around Sheena's shoulders, turned, and looked at her confused, the tears streaming down her face.

"What do you mean by Alan?"

"I never want to see him again as long as I live!"

"What are you talking about?"

Sheena looked up to him and began to explain; her tone was bitter. As he listens, he went cold all over and was stunned, unable to respond for a moment.

"My father is behind all of this. Where is he now?" he asked furiously.

"I don't know."

Sheena stared at him, eyes wide with surprise at the strength of his reaction.

"I know Alan. Whatever he has told you, don't listen. He's doing what my father is telling him to do."

"Did he touch you?"

"Yes." She nodded.

"What did you do when he touched you?"

"I slapped him."

"Why didn't you call me again?"

"I didn't want to worry you."

"That's not the point, Sheena. Alan doesn't believe in love, romance, or marriage."

He moved close, stroked her hair, and kissed her forehead, holding her face in his hands.

Sheena stared at him with doubts written on her face about what Alan had said.

"I love you, Sheena."

"I know the trouble Alan and my father can cause, but you must remember that I love you Sheena, *you*! You have nothing to worry about. We will get through this."

She turned toward Jonathan, and he captured her mouth with his, kissing her softly. He wanted to lay her down across the bed, but he pulled himself back from her.

"I'm here. I will look after you. Please don't cry. I'm here for you. You need to get some rest," he said. "I will be downstairs if you need me."

"It's not going to get any easier is it?" she asked sadly.

"*No!*" he nodded. "No. It's not," despondently said Jonathan, moving her hair away from her face. "We are to take these moments, Sheena, right. What my father is doing is not important because no matter what happens, I want you."

Sheena made a little murmur of happiness. He kissed the softness of her neck before he added, "I love everything about you."

At a later time that night, back at the Samson mansion, there was no one at the house except Alan. A few seconds after, Jonathan stopped off at his home. Alan was about to pour himself a glass of brandy when Jonathan entered the lounge.

"Stay well away from Sheena, do you understand?" said Jonathan, warning him.

"Sure!" responded Alan with a sarcastic smile.

"Boy! I thought we were friends. I can't believe you sided up with my father. This is another side. I never thought you would and go so low!"

Alan turned away to take his drink; Jonathan walked over to front him in person.

"Do you understand?" repeated Jonathan. "Keep far away from her. I know you have been trying. But no more, or you will regret it," he whispered with such menace.

"Didn't she tell you?" Alan's lips smiled. "Why, the second time we met, she almost gave herself to me."

His hand disappeared into his jacket pocket; he pulled out from his pocket a packet of cigarette. He pulled one out and tapped it on the table beside him before lighting it.

"That's a lie!"

"Oh no, Jonathan. I never lie. She nearly swooned into my arms. I think she likes me."

Jonathan stared at him, trying to control his anger, while Alan took a few drags.

"You're wrong about her. You think she's sweet and innocent? Well, she isn't. She's not your type. She's like all the other women who are after your money."

Jonathan wanted to leap at him, but he did not. Alan blew out a cloud of smoke.

"You're wrong. She knows you now."

"Does it bother you?"

"No! I'm not going to fight you," he said. "There's nothing here for you, Alan, just pack your bags tomorrow and leave!" Then he walked away.

Steven later found Alan alone in the lounge drinking. He took a glass and walked over to him.

"How did it go?" Steven asked with a smile on his face.

"The deal's off. I'm not going to continue anymore. I can't ruin my friendship. It's not worth it."

"Where are you going?"

"To see Jonathan. I can't do it."

"You can't!"

"No. I can't," he responded, "find someone else to do it."

Grace felt the atmosphere within the home not as cheerful as it used to be. She decided to do something that would lighten up the atmosphere. Traditionally, by the beginning of every summer, a masquerade party is usually celebrated. Therefore, she could only decide but to give one the following weekend. Many guests were invited.

CHAPTER SIXTEEN

 dozen people came to the housewarming masquerade party that Saturday. Jonathan was in his room with his mother, and Steven was in the lounge, gazing up at his grandfather's portrait. A gray-haired butler, who had been with the Samsons ever since he married, brought on a silver tray a glass of red wine. Steven took the glass of wine in his hand as the servant withdrew. He raised his glass and said, "To you, old man!"

He drank a little of the wine, then he placed the glass down on a small table beside him and walked off while a fleet of cars arrived. In the meantime, Jonathan did not feel like going to the masquerade party.

"It's almost full," Grace said as she entered Jonathan's room.

"You look stunning!" Jonathan said.

"Thank you. You look handsome yourself," she said.

"I wish we could cancel this dinner party," Jonathan said

"This whole masquerade party was your father's idea."

"Listen, I am sorry I have been a jerk lately."

"I know. This was always his favourite party of the year, but once your father has made up his mind on something, you just cannot stop him, and this is why I love him."

"I have always wanted one thing from my father . . . his attention, Mother. I have done everything to please him, and yet I have never heard him say once . . . he is proud of me." Jonathan did not want to make his father angry. Nonetheless, he was, and for this reason, Jonathan found himself becoming upset. "Why can't he be there for me? Why can't he be like a regular normal father? Why can't he be normal? Oh, forget it! I'm a failure in everything . . . Come on, put your mask on, Mother, and let's just go out there and pretend to have some fun," Jonathan said.

Grace went down, joining her guests as they were arriving. The masquerade party was going well. Grace was a charming hostess to her guests, and she enjoyed the way her guests reacted to her. She approached one of the women who was married to an important man. She was younger than her husband. Grace introduced herself.

"I'm happy that you both came," Grace said.

Sylvie smiled. "I have been hearing a great deal about you."

"Nothing bad, I hope," Grace said, smiling.

"Oh, Grace, this is so tasty. You have made such a good banquet."

"Here's an interesting morsel."

Sylvie tasted it and said with a kind face, "It's delicious."

Her husband cut into the conversation. "It's a beautiful party, Grace."

"Thank you."

Jonathan saw Alan at the masquerade party.

"What the hell are you doing here?" Jonathan snapped.

Alan swallowed.

"I asked you what you are doing here."

"I have been trying to reach you on the phone," he replied.

"Maybe because I didn't want to talk to you, so I turned my phone off. What is it that you want from me," Jonathan said. "Just go back to Seattle," he snapped, not looking at him.

"I'm so sorry about Sheena. You have every right to be angry. I will try to make it right. You're my best friend," Alan said quietly.

"You want to be friends? Great! We're friends. Now get out!" Jonathan exclaimed.

"I don't know what else to say to you, Jonathan."

Jonathan stared at him. "There's nothing you can say," he said. "You had it all planned from the start. It's not Sheena who's after the money, but you!" Jonathan said. "Anyway, I don't really want to talk about it now. I have important things to do."

Grace noticed from across the room that there was something wrong between Jonathan and Alan. She walked over to Jonathan and then said, "What's the matter? You're upset about something?"

"Not now, Mother," he responded and walked away with anger.

Jonathan saw his father leaving the room. He followed him. As he made his way down the hallway, Steven disappeared into a big room. He followed him until he overheard his father talking to someone behind the door that was left slightly open.

"Why did you hide your secret from us all?"

Jonathan entered the room, asking him who he was talking to. He noticed there was no one else in the room but his father. He looked at his father for a moment before he asked.

"What exactly did you spread around?"

"What are you talking about?"

"Think about it . . . my engagement," he pointed out.

"Oh yeah . . . that you were engaged to be married," Steven responded with sense of guilt.

"Why don't you stop lying!" he yelled.

Steven placed his glass on a small table beside him and walked up to Jonathan. Jonathan looked at his father. "Don't you know how important this story is to me?" he said, trying to convince him to reflect.

"Don't you have any idea what you're saying!" he barked. "Do you understand what you're doing? You're throwing your whole life away!"

Jonathan tried to hold back his feelings, but a surge of anger erupted, "No!" he cried out. "Don't you get it? Don't you understand? What more proof do you need? You saw your mother's medical records!" Jonathan said, trying to convince him. "I love her, and I am going to do what I said. I'm going to marry her leaving *you* and the whole lot that goes with it!"

He spoke in such a firm manner that his father looked at him in surprise. For the first time,

Steven realized he was not speaking to a boy, but to a grown-up man who knew his own mind.

Grace clamped her hand over her mouth.

"But, Jonathan, this is your home."

"No one is going to stop me. Not you, not anyone!" Jonathan exclaimed.

Grace's arms stretched out pleading to him.

"No!" he yelled. "Won't you just stop? I'm leaving tonight. He's not going to change his ways, Mother."

Grace began to cry, dried streaks of tears and blotches of black eyeliner ran down her face. She turned and stormed out the room, leaving the two who continued fighting.

"It is very important for your own sake and the sake of the family that you marry the right person."

"That is exactly what I intend to do. And whatever you want to do or say won't really matter to me at all. Nobody is going to stop me from marrying her."

A few seconds later, Jonathan walked upstairs and could hear, standing behind the door, the sound of his mother sobbing. He stood there in silence and placed his hand on the door. He never meant to hurt anybody, especially his mother. He felt guilty. He knew he could not forgive himself, but he had no choice.

He grabbed his jacket and made his way down the stairs and walked out the front door with luggage in his hand. He made his way to his jeep, slammed the door shut, and bent his head against the steering-wheel. Steven walked into the room and saw Grace clutching a picture of her son crying. He asked himself, reflecting if he had made a mistake. He sat by her side on the bed and tried to talk to her. In the meanwhile, Jonathan thought to himself, *I should have thought of this earlier*. After several minutes, he started his jeep and was about to speed off when Steven walked out.

"Listen, son, I did all this because you're my only son, and I want what's best for you like any father," Steven said, trying to reason with him. "Jonathan, I know now I have been very cruel to you, and I ask for your forgiveness. If only I knew the truth from the start. I was told that my mother committed suicide because my father kept a secret . . . a secret that brought scandal to the family name."

"I know," said Jonathan. "I know the whole story and why she died, but it still doesn't give you the right to treat these people for things that happened in the past."

"You knew?" Steven said surprisingly.

"Yes, letters were written by my grandfather," answered Jonathan as he was getting out the jeep.

"It will take some time for me to come to terms to the facts about the truth, and I promise I will never hurt her again. I hope you can forgive me. I'm really sorry!"

As they walked back together into the house, Steven stopped at the front entrance and looked straight into his son's eyes. "Bring her to the house so I can tell her personally."

Jonathan's eyes grew wide; he couldn't believe it. That moment finally came. He walked up to his son and hugged him. "I am proud of who you have become, son." As they were embracing each other, the door opened, and Grace walked in and smiled. They turned around, facing Grace and started to make their way back to where the guests were. Steven was making his way across the room when Russell Taylor, a businessperson himself, walked up to Steven with a glass of champagne and held out his hand.

"Evening, Steven. Thank you for your invitation."

"I'm happy you came."

"Steven, I'd like you to meet my wife." Steven nodded toward his family.

"This is my wife, Sylvie, and this is Isabella, my daughter." There was enormous pride in his voice.

The two men walked outside to talk about business:

"Well, Steven!" exclaimed Russell. "You're right about the island. It's a magnificent place indeed. I'm in the process in obtaining land and property here too. My family and I will be your next-door neighbor. I hear you're doing pretty well for yourself!" he said, drinking his champagne. Russell continued to say, smiling in a sarcastic way, "I hear your son is with a country girl from this island."

"You're on dangerous grounds. I would remind you that you are a guest in my house, and you were not invited to make judgments. Don't at any time interfere in my family affairs. We are in business partnership together, and don't ever confuse that!" he said angrily.

"Of course, I apologize. I did not mean to be rude, I just thought . . ."

"Well, you thought wrong."

At the end of the evening, when all the guests were leaving, Grace turned around to Russell and his wife, Sylvie. "It was nice to meet you."

"It was a pleasure."

Grace took Sylvie's hand in hers and said softly, "We look forward to seeing you again." Their eyes met and stared at each other. "Yes," she said. Russell turned to Grace while Sylvie walked away with their daughter. "Will you forgive me? I know that my actions have upset your husband tremendously . . . I apologize." Grace smiled and said softly, "You're forgiven." He turned away to join his wife and daughter. As he walked, he thought, *I must be careful.*

CHAPTER SEVENTEEN

*I*n the meantime, Jonathan managed to slip away from the party to see Sheena. As he arrived at the front porch of her house, Sheena was already at the front door. Before he knocked, she opened it. She ran out, hugging him and kissing him. Her entire family joined them on the porch as he told her the good news.

"My father will never hurt you again, Sheena. I know how it was for you, I realize now, and I will always have to live with knowing I allowed that. My mother is different. She really wants to get to know you."

"Maybe one day, all adults will learn to settle their problems with love instead of hate," Kirk commented.

"All's well, ends well," said Drusilla.

"I don't think so," Coretta replied.

"He wants to personally tell you himself," announced Jonathan. "I will be with you, don't worry."

"I will go," Sheena insisted.

"NO! NO! NO! No way. You're not going anywhere," Leon protested.

"What can he possibly do to her? Let her go," stressed Glenn.

Sheena hugged her parents and walked away toward the jeep with Jonathan. An hour later, they arrived at the mansion. Jonathan guided to the front entrance. They walked along the wide corridor that led to a large room with huge gleaming white windows, where his mother would be waiting. She took a deep breath and walked in. A breeze blew through the room, moving the curtains at one end and out the other like a flag, twisting them. Jonathan, grabbing her hand, leaned over to her and murmured, "You look great. Don't worry. I won't let anything happen to you."

Before they came to a standstill, Jonathan said, "Mother, I'd like to introduce Sheena Becker." Sheena saw how attractive and elegant his mother was. She seemed much younger than her age. She wore strands of amethyst and ruby glass beads twisted into a choker around her neck and small good medallion drop earrings on her ears. "And, Sheena, this is my mother, Grace."

"I'm glad to meet you, Mrs. Samson," she said, taking his mother's outstretched hand.

"Come and sit with me. I'm Grace Richardson, but please, call me Grace." She followed her. "I have never seen a young woman like you who looks so exotic!" Grace exclaimed softly. "She is extremely lovely," she said looking at her.

"Thank you."

Jonathan got up from where he was sitting, walked across the room to the minibar, and took a bottle of mineral water from it.

"I know that Jonathan loves you very much, and certainly, I trust his judgments because I could see how much he has changed.

He has been so happy." Grace thrust out her hand. Sheena took hold of it and shook it. Grace then said, "I can think of no one I would like more to be his wife."

"Thank you."

"I'd like to get to know you better, Sheena."

"Do you both want anything?" asked Jonathan at the bar.

Sheena shook her head. Jonathan walked back, sat down next to her, and took hold of her hand before leading her away to his father's study that was filled with books, where Steven was waiting.

"Father, this is Sheena, you said you wanted to meet and talk with her." Steven was at his desk.

"Yes, Jonathan, I'm keeping my word. Let her in and leave us two alone."

"You look great, Sheena," Steven said then gave her a kiss on her cheek just before entering. While walking into the room very slowly, Sheena's nerves churned, turning her confidence shaky. She wondered what was going to happen next. He looked up as the tall, slim, young woman entered the room.

"Why am I here?" she asked as anger sparked from her eyes. "At least tell me what you want from me."

She stood halfway in the room when he tried to calm her to explain, although he knew he would fail.

"I should have known," she continued as anger still reverberated from every cell as she walked toward him.

"I would like to talk with you. Don't be afraid. I'm not going to harm you. I have no wish to do so." He moved toward her, looked up at her, and said, "I am delighted that you came. Please"—gesturing for her to take a seat—"hear me out."

She hesitated for a moment and took her seat, crossing her long shapely legs. As Steven was talking, she found it difficult to believe that he was the same person who threatened her. She stared at him in astonishment. *Was he for real?* she asked herself in her mind.

"I asked my son to bring you here before me because I owe you an apology . . . I want you to know how much I admire your character. You really are a remarkable young woman." Then he continued, "You and your family have every right to hate me. I wanted only the best for my son, that's all."

"I know."

"To tell you the truth, I'm disgusted with the way I have behaved. I wasn't thinking. I wish I could take the words back. I hope you can forgive me and my wife. But especially me on how I treated you and the way I spoke to you."

"I can't argue with that."

He rose from his seat, crossed the room in her direction, and sat himself next to her. "Do you mind if I sit here?" he asked.

"No."

Thank you. You both deserve each other. I'm ready to answer any questions you want to ask me."

"You surprise me!" said Sheena. "Why are you doing this?" she asked.

"Honestly, I knew when I saw you for the first time. When I looked into your eyes, I saw not just a very beautiful young woman, but also an honest and trustworthy, not alone a very courageous one, which my son needs."

Sheena smiled. "I'm glad!" she said.

"You're a very remarkable young woman."

"I didn't do anything special."

"Do you know the story of Helen of Troy?"

"Yes."

"Well . . ."

"Okay, I understand."

"I will start with giving you and Jonathan our blessings."

They both stood up, looking at each other. He did not say anything more. He stretched out his hand to shake hers, but Sheena walked over and hugged him. "Thank you," Sheena said quietly. Steven walked to the door and left the room, closing the door behind him. Jonathan ran across the room after hearing the good news, embracing her.

"There is one more thing I must do," she said.

"What's that?" he asked.

"I must visit my grandma."

They both set off.

Together, the two walked down the path that led to the gate of the cemetery. At one moment, Sheena glanced up at the sky. She blinked in the bright sunlight and looked away. She held Jonathan's arm as they continued on down the path, and at one moment, she said quietly, "The cycle of life is endless, and it never changes."

"What do you mean by that?" he asked.

"There has been a death within the family, and when the time is right, there will be life, a birth of a child. That's the way it is. When one soul has gone in peace, a new soul is born."

Together, they stood in silence at the grave for a few minutes, thinking of Datilda, who had died. She remembered the way she would call her and tell her stories as they sat under mango trees or on the terrace when she was a child. Leaning over, she closed her eyes and said a quick prayer before placing a bunch of fresh flowers on her grave. Lying beside her was her husband, Gilbert Becker. She wiped a stream of tears from her cheeks. Sheena came to understand that her grief would last for a long time and that she must let it run its course. Straightening, she turned to Jonathan and placed her arm around his.

"I'm glad we came," she murmured.

"I gave her my word, we would."

"Now they're together and at peace," Sheena said, "out of pain and suffering."

Jonathan nodded. "Their souls are free. She wasn't a bit afraid to die at the end."

"I think we'd better be going. It's going to take us a good half-hour drive."

Sheena turned to Jonathan and nodded as they made their way out of the cemetery. As they were walking down the path, Jonathan noticed an unusual brown-coloured bird with an orange breast, hopping along the edge of the grass, pecking at the soil. He wondered what species it was; he had never seen this kind of bird before. At the jeep, Jonathan settled himself in the driver's seat.

Sheena sat beside him. He leaned to her and kissed her cheek. "I love you, Sheena." A smile formed on her mouth as she heard the words of Jonathan. On her part, Sheena was wondering how her life would ever be the same again. Not *even*, because of Jonathan.

CHAPTER EIGHTEEN

After some time, news had spread like wildfire on the engagement between the Becker and Samson families. The Samsons decided that the two families should get together in December to share a special moment; this was the very first get-together dinner and significant occasion. As the months drew closer, the two families were worried what would be the outcome. There was no longer any question about *when*; December had arrived. The two families united after four years from Datilda's death. Sheena came out of the shower, wrapped in a towel with another wrapped round her wet hair. There was a quiet knock at the door, then it swung open. Coretta stood in the doorway. "Well, Sheena. We're all one now. Thanks to you." She walked over and kissed the top of her head and walked out with a smile on her face.

Sheena then slowly rubbed cream over her cheeks and nose. The main dining room seemed more appropriate than ever. The table was all set, and their guests arrived. Jonathan could hardly wait to see her. Looking toward the entrance door, he spotted her and walked over to meet her. As he came toward her, she looked and thought how handsome he looked. He was extremely well dressed. Grabbing her hand, he leaned over and murmured, "You look gorgeous," and that was true—she was stunning, and he gave her a perfunctory kiss on the cheek.

"Come with me," he said as he took hold of her hand, leading her toward the lounge near the fireplace. Charlotte passed by with a tray carrying glasses of white wine; Jonathan collected two. They stood, sipping their wine and staring at each other. The two sets of fathers finally met and embrace each other. It became a memorable moment for all as the first moments of the New Year began. Steven ushered everyone into the dining area. The families were gathered around the dining table with laughter floating through the air. Steven proceeded to pour wine in their glasses. Charlotte was doing everything along with her husband Delroy—seating the guests and bringing in their dishes. Grace and Coretta were chatting while Steven and Leon were laughing. As the guests finish their dessert, they all decided to dance along with the music. A half smile touched Jonathan's mouth. He rose and stretched out his arm to Sheena. She turned slightly on the chair, took her hand in his, and pulled her to her feet so that she was facing him, and they began to dance.

"This is not quite how I imagined the evening to be," Jonathan muttered.

"I thought it would end differently too," Sheena admitted, smiling. "We're both lucky."

Steven looked at Grace and thought what a beautiful woman she was. As the clock struck twelve, Steven and Leon, both took turns to ask everyone to raise a toast to a gathering of two worlds and two families. As the champagne sparkled in the candlelight, dreams and wishes were encouraged, blessings were given, and love was honored. Jonathan and Sheena's culture and heart have united and brought the opportunity to learn and to love, which comes from God, and to grow walking hand in hand together for eternity.

True love does not come by finding the perfect person
but by learning to see an imperfect person perfectly.

As Shakespeare said, "Love is blind."

Once you find someone you really love,
try your hardest not to lose them,
because you will never get over the feeling of loneliness.

A very brief part of Kerrine Peck's second two-part sequel novel coming soon, *A SHADOW OF SECRETS* . . .

*T*he two love birds finally got married, and the two families met at the mansion, lifting their glasses to this special event before Jonathan and Sheena set off on their honeymoon. Meanwhile, in another part within the area was a stranger looking around for the Samson mansion. He could not find where exactly; he was lost. So he immediately parked his car to the curb, switched off the engine, and sounded his horn to draw the passerby's attention. As the passerby came closer, the stranger saw it was a young boy. He asked him to guide him in the right direction. The young boy stepped forward of the stranger's voice, leaned his head, and indicated on the map. "You're way off . . . It's way back that way." He repeats the directions back to check that he understood.

The stranger looked at the direction that the passerby points. "Thank you very much. I appreciate the help."

He continued looking around until he finally found the address which was posted on the outside of an iron steel-gated property. The gates of the property opened, and a black Mercedes-Benz Viano model came out. He stared at it as it turned in his direction. The car passed beside his with the newly wedded couple and disappeared down the road. The gates were left unclosed; he advanced through the open gates and up to the driveway. His eyes scanned the property and the ground; they were lit up and looked well treated. He parked his car and stepped out. He was middle-aged, tall, five feet eight inches, tanned, with jet-black hair in a smart business suit. He walked up the steps that were leading to the front porch. Still, this was no ordinary visit. As he approached the front door, he paused only briefly. "Well, this is it," he said to himself. He lifted his hand, hesitated, then rang the bell. There was no answer. He rang again and waited. There was no answer. He stood there and rang again and waited for a response. At that moment, the two families were talking, laughing, and embracing each other. The door suddenly swung open, and a middle-aged woman stood at the doorway. It was Charlotte, the maid. The stranger gave an imposing stare. He smiled.

"Yes, can I help you?"

"Yes. Is this the Samson residence?"

"Yes, who shall I say called?"

"I'm an invited guest."

Charlotte insisted, "Please, who may I say called?" The stranger did not respond. Charlotte went to the dining room where everyone was celebrating. Grace turned and saw Charlotte and asked.

"Madam, there is a gentleman at the door, and he says he's a guest, and another thing, he won't give me his name."

"Don't worry, I will go," said Grace to her husband, and she rose from her seat, leaving her guests with her husband.

"Excuse me. I'm Mrs. Samson, Steven Samson's wife. Can I help you?"

"Aren't you going to invite me in?"

He was tall and well tanned, and the suit he wore was impeccable. His cologne was light; it crept into her nostrils.

"Excuse me, who did you say who you were?" she asked.

"I am here on urgent matters concerning Datilda Shawn and Charles T. Samson."

"I'm sorry, but we weren't expecting anyone this evening," she explained in a kind voice. "Couldn't you come back another day?" she suggested.

"I'm sorry."

"Okay, please come in."

He was invited in. "Follow me, please." He immediately walked behind Grace down the hallway which led through another door. His eyes looked at everything in the hallway. He drew to a halt when he came across the lounge where the doors were left open. He saw a portrait of his father hanging in there on the wall. She continued toward the room were the others were. She opened the door. Steven and the rest of the entire family, including the Beckers, were all standing around a large white table. Grace addressed him. The stranger walked in, invited by Grace. Everyone turned round with smiles on their faces. As the stranger entered, there was silence.

"What can I do for you?" Steven said.

"Evening, everyone, sorry to barge in like this. There is something you all need to know that you probably don't know."

"What are you talking about?" asked Steven confused.

"If only you knew," he said in a sarcastic way.

"I hope you're not wasting my time," Steven said. "This is a personal family reunion."

"I know. I don't think it's a waste of time," he responded. "I will introduce myself, but first, it's better that you all sit down, please . . . I don't know quite how to start." ***WHO WAS THIS STRANGER THAT STARTLED THE ENTIRE FAMILY?***